SHOWING OFF

CAROL ELLIS

D1712733

SCHOLASTIC INC.
New York Toronto London Auckland Sydney

ISBN 0-590-40636-1

12 11 10 9 8 7 6 5 4 3 2 1   7 8 9/8 0 1 2/9

Printed in the U.S.A.   01

First Scholastic printing, July 1987

CHEERLEADERS
SHOWING OFF

CHEERLEADERS

CHAPTER

1

The six members of the Tarenton High Varsity Cheerleading Squad sat on the sidelines, waiting to go on. Around them, the crowds in the stands stamped their feet and yelled as the Tarenton Wolves made another basket against Garrison, which put Tarenton ahead by thirty points.

Sean Dubrow, one of the two boys on the squad, punched his fist into the air. "That's the way to do it, Wolves!" he called, as the two teams raced across the gym floor. "Now bury them!"

"I think they're already buried," Olivia Evans commented, her brown eyes crinkling in a smile. "I bet they wish they'd never shown up."

"Actually, I feel kind of sorry for them." Tara Armstrong stopped combing her long red hair and pointed to a Garrison player who'd just had the ball taken away from him. "Look at that poor guy. Did you ever see a sadder face in your life?"

"Save your sympathy," Sean told her. "He's going to look a lot sadder than that when Tarenton wins the championship in a couple of months."

"Speaking of champions," Olivia said, "come on, let's get back out there and show the Garrison squad what cheerleading is all about."

A rousing shout greeted the cheerleaders as they took the floor, and they responded to it with victorious smiles. Under the coaching of Ardith Engborg, the Tarenton squad had become the best in the tri-state region, and their routines were almost as exciting as the games they cheered for.

Olivia, her small, lean body like a coiled spring, knelt in the center of the shiny floor beside Jessica Bennett. Jessica, her long brown hair spilling over her shoulders, was the picture of concentration; she barely heard the crowd cheering them in anticipation.

On either side of them, Tara Armstrong and Hope Chang stood with their pompons aloft. Tara had forgotten about feeling sorry for Garrison, and her dazzling smile reached to the highest bleacher. Hope, her shining hair like a dark curtain around her face, lifted her chin and looked ready to fly.

Behind them, hands on their hips, were Sean, whose dark eyes glittered as if he'd just heard the best joke of his life, and tall, lanky Peter Rayman, a shy grin spreading across his face as he stood before the crowd.

Olivia, the captain, gave a slight nod, and, on cue, the squad went into action.

"Hey, Garrison, had enough?
Tarenton's winning and that's no bluff!
Look out, Garrison, life gets tough,
When the Tarenton Wolves
Are struttin' their stuff!"

With the crowd clapping along, the cheerleaders began to strut *their* stuff, moving into a
routine that was part acrobatics, part dance, and
all rhythm. Sean and Peter kept the beat with
their hands, while Hope and Tara, pompons
whirling, moved around in a jazzy dance step.
Olivia and Jessica, the best gymnasts on the
team, leaped into the air from their kneeling positions, bounded across the floor in a series of handsprings, joined the dance for a moment, and then
cartwheeled back to the boys, who lifted them
onto their shoulders.

The last maneuver drew a round of applause,
which got louder when the cheerleaders spread
out and, arms on each other's shoulders, kicked
like a chorus line.

"Look out, Garrison, life gets tough,
When the Tarenton Wolves
Are struttin' their stuff!"

"Now that's what I call a real laugher," Sean
said later, as the cheerleaders piled into a booth
at the Pizza Palace. "Ninety-eight to forty-six.
Garrison didn't stand a chance."

"I don't think anybody stands a chance,"

3

Peter remarked. "It'd take a minor miracle for anybody to catch the Wolves." Sliding into the booth next to Hope, he slipped an arm around her shoulder and pulled her closer to him. Until he'd met Hope, Peter had been almost painfully shy around girls. Around most girls, he still was, but not around Hope. With her, he'd found what he thought was the perfect relationship — she was smart, she was pretty, and most of all, he was comfortable with her.

Hope knew she cared about Peter, although she wasn't always sure they had a perfect relationship. But at the moment, she was more interested in hunger than in love. "What shall we get?" she asked everyone. "The works?"

"The works minus anchovies," Olivia said, glancing at her boyfriend, David Duffy. "Okay?"

"Okay with me," David told her. He pulled off his favorite hat, a soft, well-worn yachting cap, and put it on top of Olivia's brown hair. "You know how I feel about anchovies."

"I do?"

"Sure." Leaning close, he whispered, "As much as I'm for you, I'm against anchovies."

Laughing, Olivia squeezed his hand and turned to Jessica. "Is that okay with you?"

Jessica stopped talking to her boyfriend, Patrick Henley, long enough to nod. "It's fine," she said. "I can't *stand* anchovies. Ugh!"

And I can't stand all these romantic couples, Tara thought glumly. Olivia's got David, Hope's got Peter, and Jessica's got Patrick. And who have I got?

4

Eyeing Sean, who was sitting beside her, Tara sighed. Sean was one of the best-looking boys around. Everyone agreed on that, especially Sean himself, which was the problem — he was so sure he was every girl's idea of the perfect boy. Tara knew he wasn't perfect, but he was exciting to be with. Still, nobody got Sean Dubrow. Not that Tara really wanted him that much, or for that long. The boy she really wanted, or thought she wanted, was Bill Hadley, a star on the Tarenton basketball team. Unfortunately and unbelievably, Bill was involved with Diana Tucker, who, since transferring to Tarenton from California, had done her best to get on the Varsity Squad. She'd done her worst, too, like bad-mouthing the squad every chance she got, or trying to turn Tara against Olivia. Nothing had worked, which just made Diana more determined. And when she saw that Tara was interested in Bill, she'd swooped down and snapped him up like a falcon hooking its prey.

Tara was sure she'd find a boy someday soon, and she wasn't really too depressed about Bill. Anyone who let Diana hook him was going to get clawed, and as far as Tara was concerned, he deserved it. But with so much hand-holding and shoulder-squeezing going on around her, she was beginning to feel left out, and Tara Armstrong was not used to feeling left out.

"Hey." Sean nudged her arm, breaking into her thoughts. "I get the feeling you're not completely with us. What's on your mind?"

Tara tossed her head and shrugged. "Well, I

5

wasn't thinking about pizza, that's for sure," she said. "I was thinking about romance."

Throwing his arms out wide, Sean gave her a cocky smile. "Well, here I am, Tara," he joked. "Come and get me."

"I said *romance*," Tara told him, giving his arm a playful punch. "You don't have a romantic bone in your body."

"I'm hurt, Tara, really hurt." Sean pulled a sad face, but his eyes kept their sparkle. "I thought you, of all people, appreciated what a sensitive guy I am under all this self-confidence. Why, sunsets make me want to write poetry. . . . Show me a sad picture, and I'm ready to cry. . . . Tell me a sad story and — "

"Oh, be quiet and eat your pizza." Tara punched his arm again, but she was laughing. Sean might not be perfect, but he could almost always make her laugh. And besides, he was powerfully attractive. He'll do, she thought, until somebody else comes along.

"Well, look at this!" an overly sweet voice said. "I see the entire squad is stuffing itself. Better watch out or your routines will collapse under the extra pounds."

Tara, with a mouth full of pepperoni and cheese, looked up to see Diana, her blonde hair shining like the silk of her blouse, and her perfect mouth curved in a sarcastic smile. Slightly behind her stood Bill Hadley, tall and sandy-haired and handsome.

Swallowing quickly, Tara flashed Bill a warm

smile. "That was a great game, Bill," she said, ignoring Diana. "Everyone's sure the Wolves will take the championship this year."

"Thanks, Tara," Bill said, looking pleased with himself. "I guess we shouldn't count our chickens, but it does look pretty solid."

"If the Wolves do win, it'll be mostly because of you," Diana told him, putting a possessive hand on his shoulder. Turning to the others, she said, "Bill's going to be famous sooner than that, though."

"What's he going to do, win the lottery?" Sean asked.

"Something much better than that," Diana said with a smirk. "Look behind you."

Turning, the cheerleaders glanced at the wall next to their booth. A large poster, with a drawing of an impossibly good-looking young man on it, proclaimed: YOUNG MR. TARENTON. HE'S FRIENDLY. HE'S BRIGHT. HE'S HANDSOME. HE COULD BE YOU. IF YOU'RE 16–18 YEARS OLD, ENTER THE YOUNG MR. TARENTON CONTEST. YOU MIGHT COME OUT A WINNER.

"A beauty contest?" Olivia almost choked on her Coke. "For boys? I never thought I'd see anything like that in my life!"

"It's *not* a beauty pageant," Diana said indignantly. "And there's nothing ridiculous about being a winner." She started to say more, but the cheerleaders were laughing so hard they wouldn't have heard her, so she grabbed Bill's hand and pulled him away in a huff.

7

"I always suspected Hadley was a jerk," Sean said, when the laughter had died down. "And now I know. A beauty contest — can you believe it?"

"I wonder if they'll have to parade around in swimsuits," Jessica said thoughtfully.

"Now that's not such a bad idea," Tara remarked with a laugh. "Maybe I'll go."

"Let's all go," Olivia suggested. "We can whistle and stamp our feet when they walk down the runway!"

"I hate to spoil the fun," David said, "but I'm afraid there's no swimsuit competition."

"You mean you know about it?" Olivia asked.

David nodded, looking slightly embarrassed. "To tell the truth, I have to cover it." A student at the junior college, David worked part-time as a reporter for the *Tarenton Lighter*. "I had the same reaction you did," he said. "It just wasn't my idea of a real challenging story. But my boss said there was nobody else to cover it, and since I'm low person on the totem pole, I decided I'd better not argue."

"So whose bright idea was this Young Mr. Tarenton Contest?" Peter asked.

"I don't know for sure, but a bunch of businesses in the area are putting up the money," David told him. "Anyway, like I said, there's no swimsuit parade. But there is a talent contest."

"I wonder what Bill Hadley will do for that," Sean said with a grin. "Shoot baskets?"

"I still don't get it," Hope said. "Is this just a talent show?"

8

"I haven't checked all the rules yet," David told her, "but to enter, a guy has to have a certain grade point average. A 'B,' I think." David grinned. "After all, he's Young Mr. Tarenton, so he can't be just any slob who's flunking out."

"I still think the whole thing's ridiculous," Olivia said, reaching for another slice of pizza.

"Ah, but you haven't heard what the prize is," David said.

"Don't tell me," Jessica said. "A meeting with the mayor and a key to the city?"

"A year's supply of aftershave?" Patrick suggested.

"Free passes to the movies?" Hope guessed.

"More," David told them. "Much more."

"A scholarship?" Peter said.

"Nope. But that's more in the ball park."

"I've got it." Sean snapped his fingers. "Cold, hard cash, right?"

"Close," David agreed. "Actually, if I could carry a tune or tap-dance, I would seriously consider entering."

"You're kidding," Olivia said. "It must be some prize."

"It is," David said. "An all-expense-paid trip to Hawaii, land of palm trees, pineapples, and beautiful beaches."

Sean gave a low whistle. "Not bad," he said. "Not bad at all."

"The trip is chaperoned, of course," David went on, "because — and this is the best part — it's an all-expenses-paid trip for two. And Mr.

9

Tarenton gets to pick the second person."

Suddenly, no one was laughing anymore. A Young Mr. Tarenton Contest might sound silly, but there was nothing silly about a trip to Hawaii.

Fantastic was more like it, Sean thought to himself: warm sand, sunny skies, and a beautiful girl to share it with him. He'd already decided to enter the contest. He knew he'd have to win before he could climb aboard that plane to Honolulu, but at the moment he was more interested in who he'd take with him. Since he wasn't involved with anyone then, that left the field wide open, just the way he liked it.

Tara, of course, was a strong possibility. She had the looks, and even though the two of them had had their battles, that kept the relationship from getting boring. And Sean would bet she'd leap at the chance. Well, he'd decide when the time came. For now, he'd just keep her — and all the other possible girls — guessing.

Beside him, Tara finished her Coke and pretended to listen to the conversation around her. But her mind was on the contest. Now she knew why Diana had been so excited about it. If Bill Hadley won, Diana would be on her way to Hawaii with him.

Glancing over at Sean, Tara narrowed her eyes and studied him. With his dark hair and eyes, and his fabulous build, Sean was the winner as far as looks went. Plus he was talented. Of course, Bill might have some hidden talent. Maybe he could sing or play a musical instrument. But if he did, Tara had never heard about it. And Sean was such a great cheerleader. All he'd have to do was perform a dynamite gymnastic routine, and he'd be hard to beat. If Sean entered and won, Tara thought, he might — no — he'd just *have* to take me with him.

CHAPTER

T̄he next morning, Saturday, Sean got up earlier than usual. When he'd made up his mind to enter that contest the night before, all he'd thought about was Hawaii. But as he was falling asleep, imagining that he heard the pounding of the surf right outside his window, he suddenly remembered that not only had he not won the contest yet, he hadn't even entered it.

Duffy hadn't been too clear about all the rules, and there might be some time limit, or some qualification that Sean didn't know about. Better get going, Dubrow, he told himself. You don't want to dream about the surf for the rest of your life — you want to swim in it.

Draining a glass of orange juice, Sean wrote a short note to his father and stuck it on the refrigerator door with a magnet shaped like a racing car. Sean's mother had died years before, so it was just the two of them in the big house now.

And they were both so busy, it sometimes seemed like the refrigerator door was their only way of communicating.

This morning, Sean knew, his father was sleeping in. He'd thought about waking him and telling him about the contest, but then he'd changed his mind. Mark Dubrow's job as a salesman for Tarenton Fabricators kept him hopping, and when he wasn't working hard, he was playing hard. Besides, Sean was pretty sure what his father would say about the contest. The two of them might not talk much, but they were usually on the same wavelength, and he knew his father would tell him to go for it.

Grabbing his jacket, Sean was just about ready to head out the door and go for it when the phone rang.

"Sean?" Tara's voice said, "I was afraid you might be asleep."

"Well, you know what they say about the early bird," Sean joked, leaning back against the kitchen wall.

Tara laughed. "Tell me, what worm are you hoping to catch?" As if I don't know, she thought.

"I'm not sure," Sean said. "What do they call worms in Hawaii?"

"They call them worms," Tara told him, laughing again. "I guess that means you've decided to take a shot at being crowned Young Mr. Tarenton."

"I'd say it's worth it, wouldn't you?" Sean asked. "Think of it, Tara — the palm trees, the moonlight walks along the beach."

Tara didn't need to be reminded. She'd been thinking about it all night long. Of course, she couldn't come right out and ask him to take her if he won the contest, because she'd never get a straight answer out of him. But she could make sure he knew she was on his side. That would appeal to his over-large ego. "I'm really glad you decided to enter," she told him. "I'll keep my fingers crossed, but I bet I won't need to. I bet you'll win."

"Thanks, Tara." Sean grinned into the phone. He knew what she was up to, but he also knew Tara. If she didn't like him, she would never have started this not-so-subtle campaign to be his companion of choice. And knowing that she liked him appealed very much to his ego. "Listen," he said, "I was just on my way out to sign up for it. Why don't I drop by your house and pick you up on the way?"

"Well. . . ." Tara pretended to think about it for a few seconds. "Okay," she said, hoping she didn't sound too eager. "Why not? It might be fun." And it just might be my first step on the way to Hawaii, she thought, hanging up the phone with a smile.

Registration for the contest was at Tarenton Town Hall, and as Sean pulled his red Fiero into a parking space half an hour later, Tara's mouth dropped open in surprise. "I've never seen so many boys in one place in my life," she said, looking at the crowds heading into the hall.

14

Sean laughed. "Looks like I'm not the only one who wants to go to Hawaii. Oh, well, this'll give me a chance to check out the competition."

Tara was just about ready to tell him he didn't have to worry, when she spotted a very familiar couple just going in the door. "I don't believe it!" she gasped. "That was Peter and Hope!"

"Couldn't be," Sean said, getting out of the car. "Rayman wouldn't enter a contest like this, not even for a million dollars."

"Sean, they've been together for ages," Tara argued. "I know what they look like. And you're right, this doesn't seem like the kind of thing Peter would be interested in. That's why I was so surprised."

"Well, don't worry about it," Sean told her as they walked across the parking lot. "Maybe they're here for something else. Come on, let's go fill out that entry form."

The inside of the hall was rapidly filling up with boys — some alone, but many more with their girl friends. Tara recognized a lot of them, including Bill Hadley, who was with Diana. A man stood at the doorway of the auditorium, passing out entry forms, and as she and Sean worked their way over to him, Tara caught a glimpse of the couple she'd seen earlier. This time, there wasn't any doubt — it was Hope Chang and Peter Rayman.

Tara started to call out to them, but one look at Peter's face made her stop. He looked miserable. Tara didn't know what was wrong, but she decided she'd better stay out of it. Hope was there, and she could do a better job than anybody of cheering him up.

Tara was right about Peter being miserable. Unfortunately, as far as Peter was concerned, Hope was the cause of it, so she could hardly be the one to cheer him up.

Why had he agreed to this? Contests were just not his thing, especially one like the Young Mr. Tarenton Contest. According to the entry form, he not only had to be talented and smart, he also had to be poised. That was a laugh. The only time he was poised was when he was cheerleading; take him out of his uniform and he was an instant Mr. Klutz, tongue-tied and red-faced. He could barely walk into a classroom of friends without blushing, so what was going to happen when he had to parade around on the town hall stage in front of hundreds of strangers?

Sighing, Peter took the pen that Hope was holding out to him and started filling in his name. When they'd left the Pizza Palace the night before, Hope had been so excited about this contest that she couldn't stop talking, and usually Hope was as quiet as he was. It turned out that she had relatives in Hawaii, relatives that she'd never met.

"It's my mother's favorite cousin," she'd explained. "And Mother's always talking about her, how funny and how beautiful she is, and how much fun they had when they were children. She has a daughter a year younger than me, but the way things are going, we'll both be old women before we ever meet."

Peter had nodded, not quite understanding what this had to do with a stupid boys' contest. Then it hit him: Hope wanted him to enter the contest so that if he won, he could take her to Hawaii with him.

"Hey, slow down," he'd said, but before he could even start to argue, Hope had pulled him into her house and announced the news to her mother. Caroline Chang, a painter and a very calm person, had actually gotten as excited as Hope. She'd immediately pulled out a scrapbook and started showing Peter pictures of her lovely cousin Joan. Then James, Hope's younger brother, got into the act, begging Hope to bring him back a toucan or at least a conch shell. Even Dr. Chang, Hope's father, wasn't his usual observant self, and didn't seem to notice that Peter was trying very hard not to panic.

Peter usually enjoyed Hope's family. They were close and loving, even if they were a little more straight-laced than he was used to. And they always made him feel welcome. Peter's mother was divorced, and she had to work so hard to pay the rent and put food on their table that she was sometimes too tired to smile. So it was always nice to go to the Changs', because the atmosphere was so different.

Last night, though, Peter just wanted to escape. But somehow — he wasn't sure how — before he'd left, he'd agreed to enter the contest. And now here he was, keeping his fingers crossed that maybe the whole thing was just a bad dream.

Unfortunately, at that moment, Peter glanced up and saw Sean and Tara waiting in line near the edge of the stage to get an entry form. So much for bad dreams, he thought. *Not only is this real, this is a nightmare.*

"Hey, Rayman!" Sean called out, taking a form and moving toward Peter. "I see we're in for some friendly rivalry." He grinned. "What are you doing for the talent part? Is Hope giving you a crash course in the violin?"

"No," Peter said, trying to joke. "I thought I'd amaze everybody with my fabulous voice." He jumped up onto the stage. Falling to his knees in the middle of the crowd, he began singing in a horrible, off-key croak. Hope and Tara climbed onto the stage also, and leaned against each other, laughing.

Peter stood up and shook his head, obviously not enjoying himself. "I guess I'll just do a gymnastic routine," he told Sean.

The three jumped off the stage and looked at Sean.

"What a coincidence," Sean commented, his eyes twinkling. "That's what I was planning on doing. Do you really think you can beat me at that?" He gave Peter a light punch in the arm and laughed, expecting him to enjoy the joke. The two of them weren't the best of friends, but they usually got along, and even though Sean was sure he was the better gymnast, he wanted Peter to know he was kidding.

18

But Peter didn't laugh. He just shrugged and put his nose into the entry form again.

"Actually," Hope said, smiling to smooth over Peter's mood, "we figured that you and Peter were such different gymnasts, it wouldn't really matter."

"Uh, yeah, I guess that's right." Sean didn't know what was bugging Peter, but he decided not to crack any more jokes. "Well, let's see," he said, checking his form. "Name. That's easy. Address and phone. Hey, this doesn't look too hard at all." Skimming down the list of questions, Sean suddenly stopped. "What's this? Community service?"

Peering over his shoulder, Tara read the form and frowned. "David Duffy didn't say anything about that."

"It means you have to be involved in the community in some way," Hope explained. "You know, like doing ongoing volunteer work at the medical center, or raising funds for some good cause — things like that."

"Oh." Sean felt a sudden sinking feeling in his stomach. All the other questions were standard: grade point average, extracurricular activities, scholastic accomplishments. But community involvement? Sean thought long and hard, but the only thing he could remember ever doing for Tarenton — apart from the time the cheerleaders had won a trip to New Orleans for raising funds for the local medical center — was selling raffle tickets to help buy a new swing set for the park. Since he'd been all of eight years old at the time, he had a feeling that wouldn't count for much.

19

Besides, he hadn't been doing it for the swing set. No way. He'd sold as many raffle tickets as he could because he'd wanted the prize — a brand new bicycle.

"Sean?" Tara was looking at him curiously. "What's the problem?"

Sean took out a pen and started filling in the blanks. The preliminary contest, where they'd pick the finalists, was ten days away. He'd come up with something more ongoing than the medical center fund-raising by them. "No problem," he told Tara. "No problem at all. Come on, let's hit The Pancake House. I only had orange juice for breakfast."

"Great, I'm starving." Tara turned to Hope and Peter. "You guys want to come, too?"

Hope started to say yes, but Peter broke in before she could get the word out. "I don't think so," he said. "I've suddenly lost my appetite. But thanks anyway."

"Oh. Well, okay." Tara was just as glad. Peter was in a terrible mood, and besides, she wanted to discuss a gymnastic routine with Sean. If she helped him with his talent routine and he won, he'd have to be grateful. "We'll see you at the game tonight, then."

After Sean and Tara left, Peter pushed his way through the crowd of would-be Young Mr. Tarentons and handed his form in. Then, not bothering to take Hope's hand as he usually did, he headed for the door.

"Peter!" Hope practically had to run to catch up with him. "What's the matter with you?"

Reluctantly, Peter stopped. "This just isn't my kind of scene, Hope."

"The contest?" Hope nodded. "I understand that, and I want you to know I really appreciate your entering." Smiling, she slipped a hand into his jacket pocket. "Not many guys would do that just because their girl friends asked them to."

Right, Peter thought. But this chump did. "I'm not going to win, Hope, you know that."

"I do not, and neither do you."

"I'm going to look like a fool," he said.

"That's not true, either," Hope argued. "Look, I know all about being up on a stage. I can give you lots of hints on how to handle it."

"That's not the same thing," Peter said. "You play the violin because you love it, so you don't mind performing in front of lots of people. I don't exactly love the idea of being in the Young Mr. Tarenton Contest."

"You tried out for cheerleading," Hope pointed out. "You didn't mind that."

"I hated every minute of it. But I did it because I really wanted to."

"Then what are you saying, Peter?" Hope asked.

She was staring at him, a confused look in her dark eyes, and Peter realized how much she meant to him. Of course, it would have been nice if she hadn't decided to change his life this way, if their relationship could just stay on its nice, comfortable, even keel. But Hope really wanted this, and he'd already agreed to go along with it.

"Never mind," he said, squeezing her hand and

21

trying to look cheerful. "I've just got a case of cold feet."

"Then I'll have to help you warm them up." Laughing, Hope put her arms around him and gave him a kiss. "You'll see, Peter, it won't be bad at all. Really, it might turn out to be a lot of fun."

Sure, Peter thought as they headed for his car. And if I really wish hard, maybe Hope's cousin will pay her a surprise visit in the next ten days.

CHAPTER

3

Saturday night, right before the game, Olivia, Jessica, Tara, and Hope got into their uniforms quickly and rushed into the small room where the cheerleaders always waited before making their big entrance.

"Does everybody know their lines?" Tara whispered, trying not to laugh too loudly.

"How could I forget them?" Jessica said. "It's the worst cheer ever written."

"That's what makes it fun," Tara told her.

Olivia, waiting by the door, suddenly held up her hand. "Quick, here they come! Get ready!"

Hope turned out the light, and with a lot of stifled giggles, the four girls crouched in the center of the floor, their pompons rustling as they tried to keep quiet.

Footsteps sounded out in the hall leading to the boys' locker room, and then they heard Sean's voice. "It's that community involvement thing that's got me stumped right now," he was saying. "Otherwise, I'd say it was in the — hey, why's it so dark in here?"

Sean reached out and flipped on the hall light, and as he did, the four girls leaped through the door, shaking their pompons and shouting.

> "Here they are,
> They're the ones
> Who want to be
> Young Mr. Tarenton!"

Quickly, they encircled Sean, kneeling and holding their arms up to him.

> "Sean Dubrow,
> he's so fine!
> The judge'll think
> he's just divine!"

Next, they formed a circle around Peter.

> "Peter Rayman,
> he's so neat!
> He's gonna be really
> hard to beat!"

Laughing hard, the four girls dashed back to the center of the hall.

> "Here they are,
> But who's the one
> Who'll wear the crown

Of Young Mr. Tarenton?
Yeah, Tarenton!"

"All right!" Sean said, clapping his hands and laughing along with them. "I'd say we've already got a head start on the rest of them. Who else has their own cheerleading squad, right Peter?"

"Right." Peter smiled, but even though his heart wasn't in it, nobody seemed to notice. Everyone was laughing too hard and busy cracking jokes about the "tuxedo competition."

"I mean, all the girls' pageants have evening gown competitions," Olivia said. "So you guys'll have to be judged on how well you wear a black tie and tails."

"Go ahead and make fun," Sean told her. "You won't think it's so funny when I'm lounging on a beach in Hawaii."

"You?" Jessica said. "What about Peter? Remember, 'he's so neat, he's hard to beat!' "

Jessica and Olivia couldn't help teasing both boys, but actually they were almost as excited as Hope and Tara. It seemed like nothing special or different had happened in a long time. There'd been the wedding, of course, of Mary Ellen Kirkwood and Pres Tilford, two former cheerleaders. But that seemed like ages ago. Pres was working at his father's company, and Mary Ellen had quit her job at the day-care center so she could work part-time at Marnie's boutique and go to college part-time. The excitement was over, and things had settled back into their old routine. Olivia and Jessica went to school, cheered at the games, and went out for pizza with David and Patrick. They weren't bored, but it was always fun when something different came along, and the Young Mr. Tarenton Contest certainly was different.

"I'm not surprised that Sean entered," Olivia remarked, as they gathered their pompons and got ready to go into the gym, "but when Tara told me that Peter was entering, too, I couldn't believe it."

"Believe it," Peter said shortly. "Hope wants to go to Hawaii. She's got relatives there."

"Well, listen, Hope, I've got an idea." With a teasing glance at Peter, Sean slipped an arm around Hope's slim shoulders. "If Rayman here loses, maybe I'll take you."

"You'll have to win first," Hope reminded him with a laugh.

"Piece of cake," Sean said confidently. Inside, though, he wasn't so sure. He still had to do a good deed for Tarenton, or he might not even qualify.

Tara knew he was worried about that. Fortunately, she thought she'd found the answer. When the game — which Tarenton won 76–60 — was over, she took Sean aside before he went back to the locker room to shower.

"Look at this," she said, handing him a small newspaper article. "I think it's going to solve your problem."

Taking the article, Sean leaned against the wall and started to read. "Wait a minute," he said almost immediately. "This is about some after-school sports program for grade-school kids."

26

"Keep reading," Tara told him.

"Okay, but. . . ." Sean read on. "Oh, I get it. They need volunteers. 'Retirees, housewives, and high school and college students are urged to volunteer their time and energy to the Tarenton Elementary School Sports Clinic.' What is it, some kind of kiddie Olympic training?"

"No, it's just a sports program for kids who either didn't make a team, or want some extra help, or don't have anywhere to go after school," Tara explained.

"Sounds like a baby-sitting service," Sean said doubtfully. "I don't think I'm the ideal type for that."

"Why not?" Tara argued. "There must be plenty of kids who'd like to learn a few gymnastic moves. Who could teach them better than you? Besides," she went on, "it's all voluntary, and it's helping the little kids of Tarenton. I think it's the perfect answer to your problem."

"Yeah, I'm beginning to see your point," Sean said, a cocky smile spreading across his face. "Big Brother Dubrow. I kind of like the sound of that."

"I thought you would." Tara laughed. "So now you're all set, right? You're talented, your grades are good, you've got poise, and you give unselfishly of your time and energy to the Tarenton Elementary School Sports Clinic."

"All right!" Sean said, doing an exuberant straddle jump in the middle of the hallway. "Get ready, Hawaii!"

* * *

27

On Monday after cheerleading practice, Sean took a one-minute shower, dressed in a flash, and rushed outside to his car, in a hurry to get to the sports clinic and put his name on the list of volunteers.

Nobody on the squad was fooled for a minute by his sudden urge to become involved in the community, and he'd had to listen to a lot of jokes, but that didn't bother him. So what if he had an ulterior motive? He was still volunteering his time, wasn't he?

And it was pretty valuable time, too, he thought, as he drove toward Tarenton Elementary School. After all, he could be cracking the books, or working on his routine for the contest, or, best of all, heading toward the lake with a great-looking girl sitting next to him. This sports clinic was a true sacrifice, as far as he was concerned.

Stop complaining, Dubrow, he told himself. A few hours in a gym are definitely worth it if they'll help you get to Hawaii. Confident that he could handle it, Sean parked his car and let himself into the elementary school gym.

The place was in chaos, or so it looked. At one end, a group of kids about three feet tall was trying to shoot baskets. Another group was learning to shinny up a couple of thick ropes hanging from the ceiling. A third bunch of kids was working their way through an obstacle course of tires and tubes and low wooden benches that they had to jump over. There must have been forty kids in all, and they all had their mouths wide open, laughing, shouting, screaming, and sometimes crying.

Wishing he'd brought ear plugs, Sean walked over to a tired-looking man who was busy checking lists.

"Hi," Sean said, raising his voice to be heard over the noise. "Are you in charge here?"

"So they tell me," the man said, running his hand through his hair. "What can I do for you?"

"I came to sign up for volunteer work," Sean told him.

"Great!" The man suddenly looked more energetic. "We need everybody we can get." Fishing through his papers, he stuck a form in Sean's hand. "Here, just fill this out and you can get started."

"Today?" Sean asked.

"Why not? What are you interested in — basketball, track?"

"Well, I'm a cheerleader," Sean said. "And I know a lot of gymnastic moves, so maybe I could do that."

"Terrific!" The man was very enthusiastic now. "So far, nobody's volunteered to do that, and the kids love it. You go ahead and fill out that form and I'll round up a group for you." Trotting into the center of the gym, he gave a piercing blast with his whistle to get everybody's attention.

Sean hadn't really expected to get started today, but then he decided it wasn't such a bad idea. The more hours he put in, the better it would look.

Soon the man was back, with seven kids trailing behind him. Clapping Sean on the shoulder, he said, "Here's your team. Good luck." Then he went back to his paperwork.

Sean faced his "team" of five girls and two boys. "Okay," he said, clapping his hands like Coach Engborg. "The first rule of gymnastics is: Don't do anything until you warm up. Spread out in a line. Give each other plenty of room."

As the kids were spreading out, a basketball came bouncing by. Sean grabbed it easily and looked around for someone to toss it to.

"Over here," a voice called.

Sean turned and saw a girl about his age watching him. She was as tall as he was, with long, strong legs; frizzy brown hair; and wire-rimmed glasses slipping down her nose. Tapping her foot impatiently, she held out her arms for the ball. "Well?"

Sean tossed the ball to her and turned back to his team, who was looking at him expectantly. "Okay," he said, "the first thing is to stretch your legs."

"Hey," the girl said, tucking the ball under one arm and walking over to him. "You're in the line of fire here. If you don't want a lot of basketballs coming your way, I suggest you find another spot."

Now that she was up close, Sean could see the freckles on her face, and the sharp brown eyes behind her glasses. She wasn't exactly his type, but that didn't bother him. What bothered him was her attitude — the way she stood there in her yellow shorts and sweat shirt, expecting him to scurry out of her way.

Glancing casually around the gym, Sean shrugged. "Sorry," he said. "I don't see any other spot. I guess we'll take our chances."

Bouncing the ball at her feet a couple of times, the girl shrugged, too. "Suit yourself," she told him. "But don't say I didn't warn you." Then she trotted back to her group of kids.

Not only does she have frizzy hair and freckles, Sean thought, she has a big mouth. Deciding to have as little to do with her as possible, Sean began leading his group through a series of leg stretches, sit-ups, and toe-touches. Three times the basketball came whizzing by, and Sean did his best to ignore it.

"All right," he said, when he saw that the kids were getting bored with warming up. "Let's get a mat out here and we'll do some forward rolls."

The eight of them were dragging the mat away from the wall when the basketball bounced across it, followed by the girl. She caught the ball, stopped, and eyed the mat.

"I don't think there's going to be room for that," she said. "We're just about ready to try a game."

"Well, we're just about ready to try some forward rolls," Sean told her. "And you can't do those without a mat."

"Forward rolls?" For the first time, she smiled, her brown eyes twinkling behind the glasses. "Are you a gymnast?"

31

Thinking she was impressed, Sean smiled back. "Not really," he admitted. "But I know something about it. I'm a cheerleader at Tarenton High."

"Oh." She nodded, her smile disappearing. "Tarenton. You beat us bad a couple of weeks ago. I go to St. Cloud," she said, mentioning a school near Tarenton. "My name's Kate, by the way. Kate Harmon."

"I think I remember that game," Sean said, telling her his name. "Were you there?"

"Sure. I go to most of the games."

"Then you must have seen me."

"Well, I saw a bunch of people in red and white uniforms running around yelling," Kate said, "but mostly I kept my eye on the game."

Insulted, Sean crossed his arms and studied her. "Do you play basketball?"

"No, I didn't make the team," Kate said frankly.

"Too bad," Sean said, not feeling bad at all. "Maybe next year."

"Umm." Kate nodded, pushed her glasses up on her nose, and kicked lightly at the mat with the toe of her sneaker. "So? Where are you going to put this?"

Still annoyed at having cheerleading described as a bunch of people running around yelling, Sean put his foot on the mat and gave it a strong push. "Right here," he said, as the mat partially unrolled. "I guess you'll just have to play around us."

Turning back to his group of kids, Sean clapped

his hands again. "Okay, everybody, we'll do some forward rolls in a minute, but first I want to show you a move that every one of you is going to learn before I'm through with you. It's called a straddle jump." Crouching slightly, Sean leaped into the air, his arms and legs spread, his fingertips touching his toes.

Sean didn't really expect these little kids to learn a straddle jump. That jump had been for Kate Harmon. She rubbed him the wrong way, like scratchy wool on his skin, but for some strange reason he felt like showing off. He did another jump for good measure, and grinned as his group applauded him. Then he turned and checked to see who else had been watching.

Plenty of people had seen him, he could tell by the admiring looks on their faces, but Kate Harmon wasn't one of them. Glasses slipping again, she was busy refereeing an argument between two of her players.

Forget it, Sean told himself. Don't bother trying to impress a girl you don't even like. That's not what you're here for. You're here to put in your time, win the contest, and then split. In a few more weeks, you won't even remember Kate Harmon.

Then, as Sean started his group on their forward rolls, the basketball once again came bounding toward the mat. Watching it go by, Sean had a sinking feeling that these were going to be the longest few weeks of his life.

CHAPTER

"Way out front
And standing tall,
The Tarenton Wolves
Are on the ball!"

"Hold it!" Ardith Engborg, the small blonde-haired coach of the Tarenton Varsity Squad, clapped her hands and shook her head. "Your pacing's way off," she told the cheerleaders. "You know this cheer backward and forward, so why are you getting so sloppy?"

"I guess we're just too used to it," Olivia said. "We do it so often."

"Right," Sean agreed. "After all, Tarenton's been winning so many games, we're beginning to sound like a broken record."

"That's a pretty poor excuse," their coach commented. "You mean you're getting so bored cheering for a winner that you think you can't make mistakes?"

"Not exactly," Olivia said sheepishly. "I guess we just got a little too sure of ourselves."

"Well, I have a remedy for that," Coach Engborg told them. "We'll just keep on doing it until you get it right. Get in position, please. And this time, concentrate!"

For another half hour, the coach worked the squad until they'd done the cheer perfectly. When she finally let them go, they trooped tiredly off to the locker rooms, still breathing hard.

"Next time I'll keep my mouth shut," Olivia said, peeling off her sweat clothes and reaching for a fluffy orange towel. "I don't know why I even opened it in the first place."

"You were right, though," Tara told her. "Not that I want Tarenton to start losing, but I wish we could work on another cheer."

"Hey," Jessica said, stepping out of the shower. "Since the Wolves aren't going to lose, maybe we can come up with a new cheer for the championship game." She reached for a sweater the same color green as her eyes, and tugged it over her head. "Something completely new, with lots of different moves in it."

"Good idea," Olivia called out from the shower. "I'll talk to Coach Engborg about it."

Suddenly Tara noticed that Hope was still slumped on the bench in front of her locker. "What's the matter?" she asked. "Too tired to move?"

"Just about," Hope admitted, running her

35

fingers through her dark hair. "But there's no reason to change, anyway. Peter and I are going to work on his routine for the contest in just a few minutes."

"That's right!" Olivia came out of the shower and started toweling dry her damp hair. "The first part's just a week away, isn't it?"

Hope nodded. "They'll pick fifteen finalists that night, and then the final competition is two weeks later." She handed Olivia's brown corduroy pants to her and smiled. "I'm so excited, I can't stop thinking about it."

"I couldn't help noticing that Peter's not exactly jumping up and down," Jessica commented, brushing her long brown hair. "Is he nervous?"

"I guess so," Hope said. "I keep telling him he'll be fine, and he keeps telling me he's going to fall on his face."

"Sean doesn't have that problem," Tara said, pulling on a sky-blue turtleneck. "He's so sure he's going to win, I don't even think he's worked on his routine yet." She laughed, but she was slightly annoyed with Sean. After all, if he didn't let her help him with his routine, he might forget that she was his strongest supporter. And if he forgot that, he might not ask her to Hawaii with him — if he wins, of course, she reminded herself.

Deciding to talk to him about it, Tara hurried to finish dressing and planted herself outside the boys' locker room. Hope joined her in a moment, and the two of them waited together for a few minutes, until an extremely gloomy-faced Peter came out.

"Ready?" Hope put as much enthusiasm into her voice as she could, wishing that some of it would rub off on Peter.

It didn't. Peter sighed, stared at his feet, and then finally nodded. "As ready as I'll ever be," he said. "Come on, let's get it over with."

He started toward the gym, but Tara stopped him. "Is Sean almost finished?"

"Sean?" Peter shook his head. "He left twenty minutes ago for that sports clinic he volunteered for." Smiling for the first time, he shook his head again. "He looked about as excited as somebody going to the dentist's office, but he went anyway. I have to hand it to the guy — when he wants something, he's willing to make a lot of sacrifices."

Wishing Peter had the same attitude, Hope walked with him into the gym. She flipped on the lights, noticed that he was frowning, and decided to ignore it.

"Okay," she said brightly, "I think you've got the basics down, don't you? What we need to concentrate on now is polishing it."

"Right," Peter agreed. "Polish. It could sure use plenty of that."

Hope kept smiling until she thought her skin would crack. "Do you want me to clap my hands or tap my foot or something, to keep the beat?"

"Whatever you think." Taking a deep breath, Peter walked to the center of the floor and stood with his legs apart, his hands on his hips.

Hope was the kind of person who rarely raised her voice — it just wasn't done in her house, no matter how angry or upset someone was. Now, though, she felt like yelling at the top of her lungs. Why was Peter making this whole thing so unpleasant? He'd agreed to do it, so why couldn't he just do it and stop acting like it was the end of the world? She thought she knew Peter. He'd always been so open and honest. But now he was miserable, and instead of talking to her about it, he'd closed up and shut her out.

For a moment, Hope was tempted to say forget it. But then she thought of how much she wanted to go to Hawaii. The Chang family was spread out all over the globe. Some were here, some were in Asia, and some were in Hawaii. Family ties meant a lot to them. Didn't Peter understand that?

Taking a deep breath herself, Hope fell back on her upbringing. You don't pick fights and you don't accuse; you accept what's given to you and you work with it. "All right," she said, "I'll clap my hands. And one, and two. . . ."

Nodding his head in time to the clapping, Peter waited until the count of five. Then, thrusting his hands into the air, he arched his back and pushed himself up and over for a perfect back flip. He did another, and then, on the third one, he wobbled. He wasn't sure how it happened, but his left foot came down wrong, his knee buckled, and he wobbled. He tried to keep his balance, but it was hopeless, and even before Hope had stopped clapping, he was sprawled out on the floor.

"Are you all right?" Hope asked.

"Umm," he grunted. He started to get up, then flopped down again. "Look, Hope, we just went through an hour and a half with Coach Engborg. I'm wiped out."

"I know," Hope said. "But Peter, I just don't know when else we can work. We've got games and workouts and studying. Plus I have to practice the violin every night for at least a couple of hours."

"I have a solution to all that," Peter said, picking himself up off the floor. "Why don't I just forget the whole —"

"Please, Peter, I don't want to hear it!" Hope broke in. Once again, she felt like screaming, and once again, she forced herself not to. "Let's just stop for today. You're tired, and I understand that. Maybe tomorrow you'll feel better. Okay?"

Peter opened his mouth to say what he'd been going to say — that he should just forget the whole thing — but, as unhappy as he was, he just couldn't. If he said that to Hope, he was really afraid he might lose her, and he wasn't ready to face that.

You're a coward, Rayman, admit it, he told himself. You'd rather let yourself be miserable than come right out and be honest with the girl you love.

With a small smile, Peter nodded. "Okay," he told Hope. "Let's call it quits for today. We'll try again tomorrow." He walked slowly toward her and took her hand. But even though they left the gym side by side, each one felt so completely isolated from the other that they could have been walking alone.

*　*　*

Gritting his teeth and pasting on a smile, Sean sauntered into the elementary school gym. This was his third visit, and he wasn't looking forward to it. The kids weren't so bad, at least. Even if they weren't very coordinated, they had a lot of energy. And they hung on every word he said, which gave him a kick.

The fly in the ointment was Kate Harmon. It was bad enough that he even had to spend his time here, but to spend his time here listening to her loud mouth was almost asking too much. The second time he'd come, for instance, he'd decided to play the gentleman and move his mat to the other end of the gym. But Kate, instead of thanking him, had just cocked her head, raised one of her eyebrows, and grinned. "What's the matter?" she'd asked. "You don't feel like dodging balls today?"

Even on the other side of the gym, Sean could hear her shouting encouragement to her group, giving them pointers on how to dribble and shoot, telling them where to stand and how to block. She was a regular sergeant, he thought, wondering why, of all the voices in the gym, he could hear hers so well.

Now, as he went inside, he saw her immediately, her glasses already steamy, her hair already starting to frizz. Didn't she ever have anything better to do? he wondered. He sure did. He knew he had to get some practice in, or he'd never make the final competition in the Young Mr. Tarenton Contest. He had his routine worked out on paper,

40

but so far he'd only had time for a couple of short workouts.

Then he had an idea. Turning to his group of little gymnasts, he clapped his hands. "Okay, guys, warm-up time," he said. "You know the routine by now, so let me see you do it on your own."

Sean watched them for a moment, counting out loud, just to make sure they did know what to do, and then, gradually, he let his voice fade out. Stepping onto the mat, he eased himself into a handstand, and from that position, he pushed off into a string of forward flips. Landing lightly on his feet, he cartwheeled back to the center of the mat, leaped into a straddle jump, did a back flip, and then a stag leap. So far, so good. All he needed now was a spectacular ending.

Too busy thinking about his final move, Sean didn't notice that his group of kids had finished their warm-ups and was standing around, waiting for him to tell them what to do. But Kate Harmon noticed.

"Nice routine," she said. "But don't you think it's a little too hard for these kids? They're not training for the Olympics, you know. They're just here to have fun."

"I wasn't planning on teaching it to them," Sean said, directing his group to start on some forward rolls. "Anyway, don't you have better things to do than stand around watching us?"

Instead of looking insulted, Kate laughed. "I gave my group a break," she said. "And it was

41

almost impossible not to notice what you were doing. You're a real show-off, aren't you?"

Sean took the bait; he couldn't help it. "For your information, that wasn't showing off," he told her. "That was practice."

"Oh?" Kate's right eyebrow shot up. "Practice for what? Some new cheerleading routine?"

"Hardly." Didn't she know that cheerleading was a team effort? "I'm in the contest, and I'm working up a routine for the talent part of it."

"What contest?"

"It's called Young Mr. Tarenton," Sean informed her. "And I know you're going to make some sarcastic remark, so don't even bother."

"The thought never entered my mind," Kate said, her eyes sparkling behind her smudged glasses. "Anyway, I heard about the prize — a trip to Hawaii, right?"

Sean nodded.

"Now I remember," she went on. "Two boys from my school are in it, too. I heard them talking about it. At least it's not a contest for complete idiots," she remarked. "I mean, your grades have to be good, don't they? And you have to be doing some kind of volunteer — "

Suddenly, Kate stopped and stared at him, her mouth slightly open, her eyes brighter than ever. "Oh, wow! Now I've figured it out!"

"Figured what out?" Sean asked, feeling like he'd just walked into a trap.

"What you're doing here," she said. "I could tell from the minute I saw you that your heart just wasn't in it. And I kept asking myself why you bothered. Now I know. You want to get to Hawaii, and you need to have this good deed on your record."

Kate looked very pleased, as if she'd just uncovered the key clue to a mystery.

To his annoyance, Sean felt a blush creep up his neck, but he forced himself to ignore it. Why should he be embarrassed, anyway? So what if Kate knew his real reason for being here? He didn't care what she thought.

"I'm sure you're dying to make jokes about this," he told her. "So go ahead and be my guest. It won't bother me at all."

"Well, I don't think it's all that amusing, actually," she said. "And anyway, it wouldn't be any fun to tease you if it didn't bother you, which I'm sure it wouldn't. I get the feeling your skin is as thick as an alligator's."

Kate turned to go, and then she stopped. "By the way," she said, "your routine needs a really great ending. Too bad you have to come down from that last leap. If you could just stay up in the air, you'd win for sure. After all, there must be a lot of talented guys in the contest, but I'll bet none of them can suspend themselves in midair." With another grin, she dashed off, her long legs taking her quickly across the floor, her voice raised in a shout that sent her group into action.

Watching her go, Sean sighed in exasperation. She's right about one thing, he told himself. I do have a thick skin. So why am I letting this girl get under it?

CHAPTER 5

Over the next few days, Sean did everything he could to keep Kate from getting under his skin. The best solution would have been to stop going to the sports clinic, but unfortunately that was out. He had to have this volunteer work under his belt, and he had a feeling it wouldn't sit too well with the judges if his record showed that he put in two or three hours and then quit.

He'd been right when he told Tara that spending time with little kids wasn't his thing, so he was actually surprised when he found himself enjoying it. Well, maybe *enjoy* was too strong a word. He didn't enjoy it all the time, but he did get a kick out of watching his group progress from the klutz stage to the point where most of them could do a front walkover, with a little help from him.

It wasn't that he suddenly decided to spend the rest of his life doing volunteer work, but still, it wasn't as bad as he'd thought it would be. And it would have been even better without Kate Harmon.

Now that she'd guessed his real reason for being there, she never missed a chance to mention it. "It won't be long now, will it Sean?" she'd say, bouncing the basketball between her feet. "When's the preliminary contest? Think you can hang in here that long?" Or, "Don't forget to tell these kids to smile. Nobody ever won a trip to Hawaii without smiling."

She'd said she wasn't going to razz him about it, but obviously she couldn't resist. The strange thing was she said all these things with a grin that lit up her face, and a laugh that was almost musical. It was as if she was daring him to laugh at himself, and Sean had to grudgingly admit that he was tempted sometimes. But he wasn't very good at laughing at himself, and he certainly wasn't going to start with this girl egging him on.

Because there was a midweek game, Sean didn't go to the clinic on Wednesday. Instead, he cheered for the Wolves, who lost for the first time in weeks. Afterward, he went out with Tara for a hamburger. Tara was on his side — most of the time anyway — and after Kate Harmon, he figured he deserved some positive female companionship.

"How's your routine coming?" Tara asked the minute they'd ordered their food. "I can't help noticing that Peter practices almost every day."

"I'm not worried about Peter," Sean said. "Besides, I've been practicing, too."

"Really? Why don't you let me see it?" Tara suggested. "Maybe I could give you some pointers."

Biting into his burger, Sean nodded. "Good idea," he mumbled. "According to this girl at the sports clinic, the ending needs to fly."

"Oh?" Tara smoothed her hair back and tried not to frown. "A girl?"

"Mmm. She goes to St. Cloud."

Tara wanted to know more. Was he interested in this girl, interested enough to take her to Hawaii? But she couldn't come right out and ask. "Is she . . . is she coming to the contest?"

"Hah." Sean shook his head and grinned. "If she did, she'd probably throw eggs at me. On her list of people she admires, I fall clear to the bottom of the page."

"Oh, well," Tara said, feeling relieved, "I guess she just doesn't know you."

Sean laughed to himself. Tara was playing her game again, trying to wangle an invitation to Hawaii out of him. He didn't mind though; he and Tara understood each other. He probably *would* ask her to Hawaii if he won, but he couldn't come right out and say it. That would take all the fun out of the game that they both played so well.

"Tell you what," he said. "Tomorrow after Coach Engborg gets through with us, I'll do my routine for you and we'll work on the ending."

Tara bit into a French fry and smiled. Even if there hadn't been any prize at all, she still would have helped Sean with the contest. But the prize did make it much more exciting, and as she ate and talked to him about his routine, she took a mental walk through her closet, trying to decide whether she had the right clothes for a trip to Hawaii.

On Friday night, the gym was filled with Tarenton students, ready to cheer their team to another victory. True, the Wolves had lost the last game, but they were still way ahead of the competition. Only Deep River was close, and they were four games behind. And tonight, Deep River was facing Garrison, usually a strong team, while Tarenton was playing a team they'd whipped just a few weeks before — St. Cloud.

When Sean realized he'd be cheering against Kate Harmon's school, he couldn't help laughing. "We're going to shine tonight, if I have anything to do with it," he said to Peter as they got into their uniforms.

"What's so special about tonight?" Peter asked.

Sean tugged his red and white sweater over his head and reached for his comb. "Tonight's special because I have an enemy at little old St. Cloud," he explained. "And I wouldn't mind seeing her team fall flat on its face."

"*Her* team?" Peter pretended to look shocked. "You've got a female enemy? I don't believe it."

"I know, I know, it's completely out of character," Sean laughed. "But you haven't met this girl. If you had, you'd understand. She's pushy. I really hate it when people are pushy, don't you?"

"As pushy as you are, Dubrow?" Peter shot back. But his heart wasn't in it. Peter had been

thinking about pushiness for quite a while. Wasn't
Hope pushing by asking him to do something that
made him miserable? Half the time he thought
she was, and he worked himself into a temper,
ready to tell her to back off. But then he always
had to admit that he'd agreed to do it, so he
really didn't have any right to complain. Which
brought him right back where he'd started —
feeling lousy and not knowing what to do about it.

"Well," Peter said now, "I think you're going
to get your wish. Tarenton's on a roll. The last
game was just a little teaser, to keep some of the
other teams thinking they might have a chance to
win. But nobody's got a chance against the Wolves
— especially St. Cloud."

At first it seemed like Peter was right. By halftime, the Wolves were ahead 36–22. The Varsity
Squad had gone through most of their "winning"
cheers, and some of the fans had actually left, deciding that the game was going to be another
laugher.

Sean had spent the first half scanning the crowd,
trying to spot Kate Harmon. She loved basketball,
he knew that much, so maybe she was here root-
ing for her team. Waste of time, Kate, he thought.
And even though he never did see her, he did
every cheer with her in mind.

Ten minutes into the second half, though, Sean
forgot about showing off in front of Kate. No one
was sure how it happened, but the St. Cloud Lions
were suddenly only eight points behind. There
was plenty of time left in the game, and if the

Lions kept it up, they just might overtake the Wolves. It would never happen, of course, everybody knew that, but the remote possibility made people scoot to the edges of their seats.

Feeling the tension in the air, the Varsity Squad took the floor and gave the crowd one of its favorite cheers.

> "Stepping high,
> Running fast,
> The Tarenton Wolves
> Are having a blast!
> Look out, St. Cloud,
> You'd better move,
> The Tarenton Wolves
> Are in the groove!
> Yeah, Tarenton!"

It wasn't one of their most difficult cheers, but it gave the crowd a chance to clap and shout along, and the fans were still making so much noise when St. Cloud got another basket that almost no one noticed it.

No one missed St. Cloud's next basket, though, or the next, and when the Lions tied the game, everyone — even the Lions' fans — looked confused, as if they couldn't quite believe what had happened.

"Okay," Olivia said, as the cheerleaders gathered at the sidelines, "we were complaining that we'd been doing the same cheers over and over. Now's our chance to do something different."

Tara frowned. "It's funny, but I can't seem to remember complaining about the cheers we do when we're behind."

"We're not behind," Sean said, wondering if it was possible for Kate Harmon to have jinxed this game. "We're tied. And Tarenton's going to win, so don't start thinking they're not."

"Sean's right," Jessica said. "Come on, let's show the Wolves we're not worried."

An argument with one of the referees gave the squad their chance. Red and white pompons whirling, they dashed onto the floor again.

> "We've got the time,
> and we've got the ball,
> Look out, Lions,
> You're about to fall!
> The Wolves are tops,
> The Wolves won't stop,
> Look out, Lions,
> You're about to flop!"

The cheer was one of their most intricate, with a complicated mixture of hand and foot movements, and a series of spectacular cartwheels by Jessica and Olivia. They did it perfectly, but unfortunately it didn't have any influence on St. Cloud.

Far from flopping, the Lions kept on playing as if they were the potential champions, and when the final buzzer sounded, they'd beaten the Wolves by two points.

* * *

50

"A minor setback," David told Olivia, as they waited for the pizza to arrive. "That's what I'm going to write in my column. 'The Wolves suffered a minor setback tonight when the St. Cloud Lions, a team of no distinction whatsoever, got lucky and found the basket one too many times.' How does that sound?"

"Good," Olivia said, shrugging off her yellow jacket. "But you sound like you're prejudiced for Tarenton. I thought reporters weren't supposed to lean."

"Guilty as charged." David's blue eyes sparkled. "I am prejudiced, and I do lean." To prove it, he leaned toward Olivia and kissed her on the cheek.

Laughing, Olivia pushed him lightly away and reached for her Coke. "Well, anyway, at least there's no game tomorrow night. The Wolves will get a rest and then they'll be back strong."

"Speaking of tomorrow night," Patrick said, reaching for Jessica's hand, "I'm afraid I can't pick you up at seven. I've got a late move scheduled and I probably won't get finished till at least nine." Patrick had his own moving business, and ever since his partner, Pres, had gone to work for his father, Patrick was working doubletime.

"That's okay." Not only did Jessica mean it, she was actually relieved. As much as she cared for Patrick, she still felt slightly smothered by him. He'd really given her a scare when Pres had married Mary Ellen, trying to convince her that they should get married, too. She'd finally made him realize that she wasn't ready for marriage, but every once in a while she got the feeling that he was just biding his time, waiting to propose again. "We can go get a quick Coke or something," she told him now.

"Oh?" David's eyebrows went up. "You mean you're deserting two of your squadmates on one of the biggest nights of their lives?"

Jessica looked confused, but Olivia laughed. "You remember, Jessica," she said. "Tomorrow night's the semifinals of the Young Mr. Tarenton Contest."

"Oh, right!" Laughing, too, Jessica looked around the Pizza Palace. "So that's why Sean and Peter aren't here tonight," she said. "I wondered why they didn't come."

"Hope told me that Peter was actually going to practice tonight." Olivia shook her head. "He must really be serious about winning this."

"He's serious, all right," Jessica commented. "He hasn't smiled since he entered the contest."

"The guy's probably nervous," Patrick said. "This just doesn't seem like his kind of thing."

"I know," Olivia agreed. Then she grinned. "On the other hand, Sean. . . ."

"Sean Dubrow was tailor-made for the Young Mr. Tarenton Contest," David finished. "You can bet he's not nervous."

"Why do you think he didn't come out with us tonight, then?" Jessica asked.

"He may not be nervous, but he's not stupid, either," David said. "He probably decided to hit the sack early tonight."

"Of course," Olivia giggled. "He's getting his beauty sleep."

"Well, I don't know about you guys, but I plan to be at town hall tomorrow night, cheering them on," David said.

"You have to be there," Olivia reminded him. "You're covering it."

"True," David admitted. "But to tell the truth, I'm kind of curious, too. Anyway, it'll be a nice change of pace from basketball games. And," he said, reaching into his jacket pocket, "I've got good seats. Any takers?"

Olivia immediately reached for a ticket. "Of course I'm going," she said. "Sean and Peter need our support. Besides, I want to see those guys go through their paces. I've been practicing my whistle for a week. What about you, Jessica?"

"Are you kidding?" Jessica laughed and took a ticket from David's outstretched hand. "I wouldn't miss that contest for the world!"

CHAPTER 6

Ten years earlier, the residents of Tarenton had voted to raise their taxes so that the town hall, which was threatening to collapse, could be rebuilt. They hadn't known about the Young Mr. Tarenton Contest, of course, but if they had, they might have decided to spend even more money and have it rebuilt at twice its original size. The hall seated five hundred, and on Saturday night, the first night of the contest, at least six hundred people were jammed into it.

"This place is a madhouse," Olivia commented, as she, David, and Jessica made their way down the crowded aisle to their seats in row D. "You'd think no one else had anything to do tonight."

"You have to admit, it's something different," David said. "I mean, how often do so many guys get together in one place and do a little showing off?"

"And how often do so many girls get a chance to see it?" Jessica asked with a laugh, as they sat down.

A thick red velvet curtain was drawn across the stage, and it rippled and billowed from the movements of the people behind it. Every once in a while, a pair of feet could be seen scurrying from one side of the stage to the other.

"I bet it's crazy back there," Olivia said. She draped her coat over the seat next to hers to keep it for Hope, while Jessica put hers over another seat for Tara. "I wonder how Peter and Sean are doing."

"Peter's chewing his fingernails," Jessica predicted with a grin. "And Sean, naturally, is flexing his muscles."

The wings and dressing rooms were roomy, but not roomy enough for the thirty or forty contestants and their thirty or forty companions. In the hall outside the dressing rooms, not only was Sean trying to warm up without bumping into anyone, but another boy was practicing a magic act, a third was tuning up his trombone, and a fourth was delivering a Shakespearean speech at the top of his lungs. The rest were scattered up and down the hall, in the dressing rooms and on the other side of the stage, practicing scales, combing their hair, and nervously cracking bad jokes.

"I just took a little walk," Tara said excitedly, coming up to Sean, "and from what I've seen, your act is going to be the one that'll knock the judges' socks off!"

55

"That's what I like to hear." Sean grinned and bent down to touch his toes.

"But listen," Tara went on, "they're going to be looking at other things besides talent, you know."

Still smiling, Sean stopped and looked at her. "Well?" he asked, turning his face in profile. "Did you see anything that compared to this on your little reconnaissance?"

"As a matter of fact, I did," Tara told him, thinking of the handsome dark-haired boy who was playing the guitar. "But I wasn't just talking about looks. I was talking about poise. You've got to be cool, Sean, but not so cool that you'll turn everybody off."

"Medium-cool." Sean nodded. "I think I can manage that."

"Make it medium-warm," Tara suggested. "You want the judges to think you're sincere."

"Don't worry," Sean told her. "When I'm finished with them, they'll think sincerity is my middle name."

"Okay, okay." Tara laughed and then stepped closer to him. "Listen," she said softly, "I heard a couple of people talking about the questions they're going to ask you. And one of them's going to be about your volunteer work."

Sean had been afraid of that. He should have known that just putting in a couple of weeks at the sports clinic wasn't going to be enough. Well, it was too late to do anything about it now. If they wanted to ask him about it, let them. He'd come up with an answer.

"All right, gentlemen," a voice said. Gradually the noise died down, and everyone turned their attention to a tuxedo-clad man.

"The master of ceremonies," Tara whispered to Sean.

With a smooth smile, the MC greeted the contestants and made a short speech about how he knew they'd all do their best. "Unfortunately," he went on, "only a dozen finalists can be selected. And from what I've seen just walking around backstage tonight, it isn't going to be an easy choice. Just give it your best shot, and remember, you're all winners."

Sure, Sean thought. But only one of us can go to Hawaii.

"Now, here's the procedure," the MC told them. "First you'll form two lines in the wings, one on stage left ; one, stage right. I have the positions here and I'll give them to you in a few moments. When the spotlight hits you, your name will be called. That's your cue to smile and walk to center stage."

"Don't forget," Tara whispered. "Warm and sincere."

"After that, you'll all be backstage again. When your name's called this time, come out, smile again, and get ready to answer some questions. Don't worry," he said, and laughed, "there's nothing tricky about them. I'll ask about your school, your extracurricular activities, your volunteer work — things like that. It'll give the judges a chance to get to know you. Following that will be the talent portion of the contest, and after that, the judges will select the finalists. Okay, good luck to you all, and let's start getting organized!"

Tara, dressed in black pants and a brilliant green sweater that matched her eyes, reached into her pocket and took something out. Keeping it in her fist, she moved even closer to Sean. "I know you're going to be great," she said, "but I brought you a good-luck charm anyway." Opening her hand, she showed him a tiny gold pin shaped like a four-leaf clover.

"Hey, thanks, Tara," Sean said, beginning to feel a little nervous in spite of himself. "Pin it on for me, would you?"

Carefully, Tara pinned the clover on his collar. Then she gave him a quick kiss. Stepping back, she smiled. "Knock 'em dead!" she said, and went out to find her seat.

At the other end of the hall, Peter stood as stiffly as a statue, ignoring the hurrying, excited people around him. Hope looked at him and felt her spirits fall another notch. She'd worn what she knew was one of his favorite outfits — a cherry-red wool sweater and matching skirt — but he hadn't even noticed. He wasn't noticing much of anything, in fact; when he wasn't staring off into space, he was watching his feet as if they were the most interesting things in the world.

Hope had tried to talk to him, not to give him pointers or suggestions, but just small talk, because she knew he was nervous. But she might as well have kept her mouth shut for all the response she got. In fact, she decided, she might as well have not even been there. Peter had obviously crawled into a shell, and he wasn't going to come out until this was over.

Taking a deep breath, she touched his arm. "Peter? I'm going to find my seat now."

"Huh?" As if he'd just waked up, Peter blinked. "Oh," he said, still blinking. "Okay. See you later."

"Yes." Hope kissed him softly, wishing he could relax. "Good luck," she whispered, and then left him alone.

Just as Tara and Hope took their seats, the lights in the auditorium dimmed, and the laughter and chatter began to die down.

"How are the two main attractions?" David asked Tara.

"Sean's fine," Tara said, "but I don't know about Peter. He looked a little — "

"Peter's fine, too," Hope broke in, a determined look in her eyes. "You'll see; he'll be great."

"I think the action's about to begin," Olivia said. "Get ready to cheer!"

There was a drumroll, and then the master of ceremonies stepped out from behind the red curtains. "Welcome, ladies and gentlemen," he said to the audience. "Tonight marks the first Young Mr. Tarenton Contest in the history of this town, and we hope it will be the first of many."

The audience clapped loudly.

"The young men backstage tonight have several qualities in common," he went on. "They're bright; they're good students; they're talented, poised, and personable; and — last but not least — they care about the town they live in, and they've shown it by giving of their time and energy to a variety of volunteer organizations."

Thinking of Sean's sudden volunteer work, Olivia held her hand over her mouth to keep from giggling. Sean had lots of good things going for him, but sacrifice wasn't one of them.

"Those are the qualities we're looking for in Young Mr. Tarenton," the MC told the crowd. "And I'm sure you'll agree that we'll find him here. Without further ado, let's meet the contestants!"

Another drumroll, and the curtain parted to reveal a single spotlight shining down on center stage. The orchestra struck up a bouncy tune, and a tall, red-haired boy walked onstage. The spotlight followed him until he reached the center, where he smiled as the MC called out his name.

For several minutes, the spotlight followed boy after boy. Some blinked in the glare, some looked slightly sheepish, and a couple raised their arms in the victory signal. No matter what they did, the audience cheered wildly, and most of them walked off the stage at a much jauntier pace than they'd walked on.

"That was Dolman," Tara said excitedly. "I'll bet Sean's next."

He was. Standing straight-shouldered and handsome, Sean waited until the spotlight picked him up. Then, his dark eyes bright, he walked confidently to center stage, waited for his name to be called, and bowed smoothly from the waist.

When he straightened up, Olivia, keeping her promise, let out a piercing whistle, and Sean acknowledged it with a grin that reached the back of the auditorium.

He did it, Tara thought, watching him stride off, his head high. He managed to be cool and warm at the same time.

More boys marched across the stage, and then it was Peter's turn. Hope gripped her hands together tightly, unable to let go long enough to clap as Peter walked quickly to the center. He nodded his head, and with only a half smile, turned on his heel and exited.

"He was a little stiff," Olivia whispered sympathetically to Hope, "but I'm sure he'll relax."

"Right," Jessica agreed. "The first part has to be the worst."

Hope nodded, still too nervous to speak.

Finally, the parade was over, and after a short wait, the MC announced that the questions would begin. Now it was Tara's turn to grip her hands together. She knew Sean was a showman, but could he pull this one off? Barely listening to the first contestant's answers, Tara closed her eyes and willed the judges to love Sean.

Whether it was the power of suggestion, or some really quick thinking on Sean's part, Tara never knew, but somehow, he was just right. If Tara hadn't known better, she would have thought that Sean Dubrow's one real regret was that he hadn't started at the sports clinic sooner.

"I guess I never gave volunteer work enough thought," he said, which was one hundred percent true. "I was always so caught up in school, and cheerleading" — he flashed his grin again " — and girls, that I didn't think there was time for anything else. But I found out there's plenty of time, and I found out that I like it."

"Thank you, Mr. Dubrow," the MC said, and to the sound of enthusiastic applause, Sean left the stage.

It was perfect, Tara thought, letting out a big sigh of relief. Sean had told the truth about when he'd started working at the clinic, but so charmingly that he came off as a busy guy who'd just discovered what a good heart he had.

"Not bad," David commented before the next boy came on. "Not bad at all."

"Bad?" Olivia shook her head in amazement. "He even had me convinced!"

"It's really kind of dishonest, though, don't you think?" Jessica asked. "I mean, we all know that Sean doesn't care about that sports clinic."

"True," David said. "But I'm willing to bet that he's not the only one of those guys who suddenly became a do-gooder."

"Probably not," Jessica agreed. "But I can't help hoping that the winner is somebody who's been volunteering a long time before he heard it might get him a trip to Hawaii."

Somebody like Peter, Hope thought, wishing his turn would come. Peter had been delivering library books to housebound invalids for ages, long before he'd heard about this contest. He was shy, and he might not be as smooth as Sean and some of the others, but he was honest and sincere,

62

and she knew the judges would like him. She just hoped he was a little looser than he had been when he took his introductory bow.

Maybe Jessica was right, though, she thought. Maybe that first walk across the stage was the hardest, and now that Peter has gotten his feet wet, he'll jump right in and swim with the rest of them.

"I'm glad I'm not one of those judges," Olivia remarked, as one of the boys left the stage. "Everybody's beginning to sound alike to me. I have a feeling that the talent competition's going to play a big part in this."

"That and looks," David reminded her. "Remember, Young Mr. Tarenton's going to have his picture plastered all over the place."

Just then, the MC called out Peter's name, and David and the four cheerleaders scooted to the edge of their seats.

Hope's heart was pounding, and even though she wasn't superstitious, she crossed her fingers.

The spotlight swept to the side of the stage, but Peter didn't step into it.

"Peter Rayman!" the MC called again.

"Where is he?" Tara wondered.

Hope shook her head, keeping her eyes on the empty spotlight.

"Look!" Olivia cried, pointing to a figure that had just emerged from the wings. "No, wait. That's not Peter."

Keeping away from the spotlight, the figure edged downstage toward the MC, handed him a note, and hurried back into the wings. The MC quickly read the note, shook his head, and then gave the audience a bright smile.

"Ladies and gentlemen, Peter Rayman has dropped out of the contest," he said. "Let's give him a round of applause, and then we'll go right on to the next contestant."

A confused murmur greeted this announcement, but most people forgot about Peter Rayman the moment the next boy entered the spotlight.

In row D, the other four turned questioningly toward Hope, wondering if she might have an explanation. But Hope sat as if frozen, staring straight ahead. There was only one person who could explain this, and suddenly Hope was out of her seat, stumbling up the dark aisle on her way to find Peter.

CHAPTER

7

"I don't get it," Sean said to Peter backstage in the dressing room. "You've already come this far. Why not stick with it to the end?"

Busy pulling on his jacket, Peter didn't even bother to glance at Sean. "Because I'm not interested," he said flatly.

"Come on." Sean grinned. "Not interested in a trip to Hawaii?"

"Not if I have to go through this to get it." Peter gave up fumbling with his zipper and finally looked at Sean. "Listen," he said, "I'm not knocking the contest. It's fine if you don't mind doing it. But it just isn't my thing."

"Yeah, I have to admit I was a little surprised when you signed up," Sean said. "But I figured you'd talked it over with Hope and decided to go ahead."

"I did, sort of," Peter admitted. "But it was a mistake. I just can't go through with it, okay?"

"Okay, okay." Sean grinned again. "It's fine with me. After all, it means one less guy to compete with."

"Right." Peter nodded, and found himself laughing. At least Sean was honest. "Anyway, good luck."

"Thanks." Sean stuck his hand out and the two of them shook. "Well, I'd better get going," he said. "The talent part's starting up and I'll be on in a few minutes. Get ready for some wild cheering!"

After Sean left, Peter finally managed to zip up his jacket, took a look around the room to make sure he hadn't forgotten anything, and then turned to the door.

Hope was standing there, her dark eyes filled with a mixture of concern and confusion.

For a moment, the two just looked at each other. Then Hope, still standing in the doorway, said, "I thought maybe you'd gotten sick."

Peter shook his head. "I'm fine."

Hope waited, but Peter didn't say anything. "Peter, aren't you going to tell me what happened?"

"You know what happened," he told her. "I quit."

"But why did you wait until now?" Hope asked. "Why did you let me get my hopes up about going to Hawaii and everything?"

"Look," Peter said, "the odds weren't great that I'd win, anyway. You saw all the other guys. Most of them were having fun; they liked getting up there on the stage and showing off. I don't."

"You don't mind cheerleading," Hope pointed out. "That's like being onstage."

Peter shook his head. "It's not the same thing at all. I love cheerleading, and when I do it, it's . . . I guess it's like when you play the violin. I sort of forget that people are staring at me. But this is different."

"It doesn't seem that different to me," Hope said. "But anyway, Peter, why did you have to wait until now to quit? It just doesn't seem fair."

"Look, Hope, I'm sorry!" Peter burst out suddenly. "I know how much your family means to you, and how much you want to go to Hawaii, but I just can't go through with this." Taking a deep breath, he looked her in the eye. "And I really don't think it was very fair of you to ask me."

"Maybe it wasn't," Hope said with annoyance. "But if you felt that way, why did you agree to do it in the first place?"

"I knew you'd ask me that," Peter said with a sigh. "All I know is I felt pushed into it. You were so excited about it — your whole family was excited about it — and nobody stopped to ask me how I felt."

"Then why didn't you *tell* us?" Hope asked.

"You didn't give me a chance," Peter said.

"That's not true!" Hope was beginning to get very angry. "And even if it was, you could have said, Hey, wait a minute, I don't want to do this."

"Well, I'm saying it now."

"You should have said it sooner!"

"All right!" Peter cried. "You're right. I should have. I didn't and I'm sorry, okay?"

"No, it's not okay!" Hope told him. "I just can't believe you did this, Peter! First you make me feel like some kind of bully for asking you to do it. Then you say you'll try but instead, you quit at the last minute!"

"Like I said, I'm sorry," Peter repeated quietly. "But I really don't understand why you're so upset — unless all you were interested in was a trip to Hawaii. And if that *is* all you were interested in, then maybe you'd better find another way to get there. And maybe you'd better find somebody else to go with you."

Hope stared at him for a moment, her hand gripping the doorknob. Then, without a word, she turned and left.

Onstage, one of the contestants was just finishing a fast-paced, impressive juggling act involving three eggs. At the end, a big smile on his face, he picked up a glass bowl and cracked each egg into it, proving to the crowd that they were the real thing. The audience cheered loudly as he left the stage, but David and the three cheerleaders in row D had hardly noticed him. They were still trying to figure out what had happened with Peter.

"I wish Hope would come back and tell us what happened," Olivia said softly as they waited for the next contestant to come on.

"I could go backstage and find out," David suggested.

"No, don't," Olivia told him. "You're supposed to be covering this. We'll find out at school on

Monday, anyway. I just hope he didn't get sick or pull a muscle warming up."

Jessica shook her head. "I have a feeling he decided to just drop out," she said. "Haven't you noticed how grumpy he's been lately?"

Thinking about it, Olivia nodded. "I guess I thought it was nerves. But maybe you're right. Maybe he really didn't want to do this." She glanced at Hope's coat, still on the seat next to her, and frowned. "Hope was really excited about this contest," she said. "If Peter did drop out, then I have a feeling she's not going to be too happy with him."

"I know," Jessica agreed. "But it was his choice, after all. And anyway, Hope didn't have some kind of guarantee that he'd win."

I don't have any guarantee, either, Tara thought. At the moment, she wasn't too concerned about Peter and Hope. Sean's turn for the talent part of the contest was coming up next, and she found herself getting more and more nervous. Sure, Sean's routine was good, but after watching ten talent acts, Tara had discovered that he had a lot of competition. The boy who'd mumbled and stammered his way through the question and answer session turned out to have a great singing voice, and the one who'd tripped and fallen during the introduction parade was completely coordinated when it came to juggling raw eggs. Tara just hoped the judges remembered all that tripping and stammering. If they didn't, then Sean's talent act would have to be more than good — it would have to be fantastic.

"Here he comes!" Olivia whispered excitedly. "Everybody clap extra loud when it's over."

Even though every contestant had his own cheering section, it was obvious from the minute Sean strode onto the stage that the entire audience thought he was someone special. He certainly looked special, straightbacked and confident, and when he made his first move — a high, graceful front handspring — the crowd erupted in spontaneous, genuine applause.

Sean was at his best that night. The other cheerleaders, who practiced with him almost every day and who knew how good he could be when he really worked at it, had never seen him like this before. There were no wobbles, no jerky steps, not a single wasted motion. From the first move to the last — the stag leap followed by the splits, which had been Tara's suggestion — the routine was flawless. Sitting on the stage at the end of his performance, his arms flung triumphantly into the air, Sean knew he'd been perfect. The audience knew it, too, and it took at least three minutes for them to stop cheering.

"I'd hate to be the guy who has to follow that act," David remarked. "I have to hand it to Sean; when he's on, he's really on!"

"It's too bad Coach Engborg didn't see him," Olivia said. "She's always telling him he could be great if he weren't so lazy. Well, tonight he was great."

"That wasn't the work of a lazy person," Jessica agreed. "He'll be one of the finalists, that's for sure, so let's just hope he can do this all over again for the finals."

"He will," Tara said, feeling like she already had one foot in the warm sand of a Hawaiian beach. "You'll see. He might not be any better than he was tonight, but he'll be just as good. And that's definitely good enough."

Although they sat politely through the rest of the talent acts, which included Bill Hadley playing the harmonica, the cheerleaders really didn't pay much attention to them. They wanted it to be over so they could go back and congratulate Sean. Whether he made the final competition or not, he'd been terrific, and they wanted to tell him so.

It was during the Shakespearean monologue that Hope came back. Trying to be inconspicuous, she slid into the row at a crouch, but Olivia saw her and smiled. "Hi," she whispered. "Everything okay?"

With a quick nod, Hope grabbed her coat. "See you Monday," she said, slipping back out of the row and up the aisle.

Everything is obviously not okay, Olivia thought, watching her go. For a moment, she wondered if she should follow her and talk to her, but then she decided not to. Hope wasn't the kind of person who'd pour out all her troubles the minute someone asked her what was wrong. She would try to work everything out by herself first. And then, if she couldn't, she might talk to somebody about it.

At that moment, talk was the furthest thing

71

from Hope's mind. Escape was what she wanted, but escape was impossible. For one thing, her father was waiting outside in the car, ready to drive her home. He was the one who had noticed that she didn't have her coat, and in his quiet but insistent way had suggested it might be a good idea if she went back for it. Why had she called him, anyway? Why hadn't she just stormed out of the building and walked home? She was too practical, that was why, she told herself furiously. Too ready to look at things logically, like the fact that her house was at least four miles from town hall, and if she walked, she'd get home so late her parents would probably ground her for a month.

Of course, the only impractical, illogical thing she'd done in a long time was to pin her hopes on Peter and the contest, and look what had happened — nothing. She was right back where she started. In fact, she was farther back from where she had started: Not only was Hawaii out of reach again, but her relationship with Peter was ruined.

At the thought of Peter, Hope tightened her lips and took a deep breath. She was still so angry that she couldn't see straight, but she knew she'd better calm down before she got in the car. If her father noticed, he'd insist that she tell him what was wrong. And there was no way she'd be able to get out of it. You didn't keep secrets from your parents, not if you were a member of the Chang family. You answered all questions, and you answered them truthfully.

Taking another deep breath, Hope forced a

smile to her lips and slid into the front seat of the car.

"I'm surprised that you're leaving early, Hope," Dr. Chang commented. "The contest can't be over yet."

"It isn't," Hope said. "But I have an awful headache, and it was so stuffy in there I had to get out." That was part of the truth, at least, she thought.

Dr. Chang nodded sympathetically. "How was it going?" he asked. "How did Peter do?"

"Not well, Father," Hope said. "Not very well at all." That was true, too. And as the car pulled away from the brightly lit town hall, she leaned her head against the cool glass of the window and sighed. "In fact, I don't think he has a chance in a million."

Forty-five minutes later, the MC stepped into the spotlight, a piece of paper in his hand and a pleased smile on his face. The buzzing of the crowd died down immediately as the audience waited to hear the list of finalists read.

"I know you're as eager as I am to learn the names on this paper," he said to the crowd. "But before I read them off, I want to explain the rules of the final competition to be held two weeks from tonight. It will consist of a talent competition, just like tonight, plus another round of questions from the judges. However, those questions will be different. Each final contestant must submit an essay explaining why he feels he's qualified to represent our town as Young Mr. Tarenton. The judges, having read those essays, will base their questions to the finalists on the contents."

"Uh-oh," Olivia whispered to David. "Sean hates writing papers. Too bad it's not going to be multiple choice."

"Don't worry about it," David whispered back. "If I know Sean, he'll turn in a dynamite essay, even if he has to pay somebody to tutor him for it."

"Remember," the MC went on, "every young man here tonight gave his best, so let's have a big round of applause for all of them!" With a sweeping motion of his hand, he gestured toward the curtain, which opened to reveal all the contestants gathered on the stage. "And now, without further ado," the MC said importantly, "let's meet the twelve finalists in the Young Mr. Tarenton Contest!"

As he called their names, each boy stepped out from the group, walked to the front of the stage, and took a bow.

No one was surprised when Sean's name was called. Tara had scooted to the edge of her seat, but she wasn't really nervous. Sean had been perfect tonight, and as he strode forward to join the other finalists, she could tell by his face that he wasn't surprised, either. He was smiling his usual cocky smile, the one that said, I'm the best. As far as Sean was concerned, the contest was already over, and he was the winner.

CHAPTER

"You were absolutely fantastic!" Tara told Sean Monday at cheerleading practice. It was probably the hundredth time she'd said it, but she didn't care. It was important to make sure Sean knew how she felt. "And that last move in your routine was perfect. I thought the audience would never stop clapping." It was also important to make sure he didn't forget that she was the one who'd helped him with that last move.

Sean grinned, enjoying the praise. "It definitely went okay," he agreed. "From here on, it's downhill all the way."

Olivia, doing some leg stretches to warm up, laughed. "Don't get too comfortable," she warned him. "Remember, you've got that essay to write."

"Piece of cake," Sean told her, touching his toes. Actually, he hadn't thought much about the essay yet. They had to be in by Friday, and he figured that Thursday night was soon enough to start worrying about it. "Those essays won't count for much. It's talent that'll win it, and it's talent I've got."

"Please, don't be so modest," Jessica commented wryly. "After all, you're with friends now, so just go ahead and let your monumental ego shine through."

With a laugh, Sean took a running leap and threw himself into a couple of handsprings, almost crashing into Peter, who was on the opposite side of the gym. "Sorry," he said, stopping himself just short of Peter's outstretched legs.

"It's okay," Peter mumbled. "Just do me a favor, will you? Talk about the contest all you want, but don't talk about it in front of Hope or me. It's not one of our favorite subjects right now."

"I'll try," Sean told him, getting ready to take another leap. "But don't feel too bad. Just tell Hope you didn't stand a chance against me, anyway." Laughing again, he gave Peter a light punch on the arm and flung himself across the gym floor.

Peter watched him go, and then, with a sigh, he went back to his warm-up exercises. If Sean had crashed into him, he thought, and broken his leg, that would have been a real favor. Then he'd be out of cheerleading for at least six weeks — and out of Hope's sight, which was the important thing.

Standing up, Peter glanced across the gym to where Hope was practicing some cartwheels. They'd been warming up for fifteen minutes, and she hadn't looked at him, hadn't even spoken a word to him. Not that Peter really wanted her to. He was still so angry that he knew talk wouldn't lead anywhere except to another argument.

He'd spent the rest of the weekend trying to convince himself that he should apologize to Hope, but the more he thought about it, the more he decided that this whole fiasco had been her fault. Sure, he shouldn't have agreed to go along with the contest, but she shouldn't have asked him to in the first place. What did she think he was, just a ticket to Hawaii? And why did she assume that he'd take *her*? There were plenty of other people who deserved a vacation. His mother, for one. Since the divorce, his mother had worked hard just to buy food and clothing and pay the rent on their tiny apartment. Never mind that taking your mother on a trip might not be the obvious choice, it still made Peter mad that Hope hadn't even thought about anyone but herself.

Sick of warming up, Peter flopped down on the floor and stared at the ceiling. Forget it, Rayman, he told himself. The more you think about it, the madder you get. It's not worth it.

Deep down inside, though, Peter knew it *was* worth it. Mad as he was, he still cared about Hope, and the thought that they might split up made him feel slightly sick — and very scared.

Scared was not the word for the way Hope was feeling. Empty was better. By practicing her violin and burying herself in homework, she'd managed to get through the rest of the weekend without her parents guessing that anything was

77

wrong. But all that work hadn't kept her from thinking about Peter. It had taken most of Sunday to get rid of that angry feeling, and now that it was gone, she just felt empty. Empty and lost.

Stop it, Hope, she ordered herself. You're not some stupid little girl who cries whenever things go wrong. You've got a brain and you know how to use it. So get busy and keep busy.

Following her own orders, Hope threw herself ferociously into her warm-up exercises. Watching her, Olivia decided again that this wasn't a good time to talk to Hope. It was obvious that something was very wrong between her and Peter, but from that look on Hope's face — that steely-eyed, determined look — Olivia knew she'd better keep her questions to herself for a while longer.

As Ardith Engborg walked briskly into the gym, Olivia just hoped that Peter and Hope would be able to cheer together. Because if sparks started to fly between them, she knew that Coach Engborg wouldn't put up with it. As far as the coach was concerned, personal problems were supposed to be left in the locker room, along with the schoolbooks and the dirty socks.

Clapping her hands, Ardith Engborg got the cheerleaders' attention and gave them a smile. "I understand congratulations are in order," she said, nodding to Sean. "I guess it's only fair to warn you, Sean, that I've already bought my ticket for the final competition, so I hope your routine is as good then as I've heard it was Saturday night."

Grinning, Sean snapped to attention and gave the coach a salute. "Don't worry, Coach," he said. "For you, I'll make it even better."

Olivia took a quick glance at Peter and Hope, but the two of them were staring straight ahead, not smiling, but not frowning, either. Good, she thought. Now let's drop the subject of the contest while everything's still under control.

Fortunately, Coach Engborg wasn't about to spend too much time on anything but cheerleading. "Okay," she told the assembled group, "the Wolves have a busy schedule coming up, and that means you'll be busy, too. Let's get going."

For the next hour, she put her squad through its paces, tapping her foot to keep them in time, urging them to jump higher, stretch farther, shout louder, and to concentrate, concentrate, concentrate. "Pretend the Wolves are two points behind with ten seconds left on the clock!" she called out. "Get that crowd on its feet!"

Remembering how the audience had cheered him Saturday night, Sean didn't have any trouble getting into the winning spirit. Tara, more positive than ever that she would soon be going to Hawaii, had so much energy that she performed her cartwheels as easily as most people walked. Olivia and Jessica, the gymnasts of the squad, leaped and tumbled and whirled as if gravity didn't have any hold over them. Which left Peter and Hope.

"Peter, you're stiff as a board! Hope, you're frowning!" Coach Engborg shouted. "Loosen up! Smile!"

A grim smile immediately appeared on Hope's face, and Peter, who was supposed to lift Olivia to his shoulders, loosened up so much he only managed to get her six inches off the ground.

Except for making him do it over again, though, Coach Engborg didn't seem to notice that Hope and Peter were functioning like robots, and after a few more minutes, she ended the practice.

"Tomorrow," she reminded them, as they headed for the locker rooms. "Same time, same place."

Sean, who was finally feeling tired, groaned when she said it, and Tara heard him. "Don't worry," she told him, "you can spend a nice, relaxing night working on that essay. I'll even help you if you like. Why don't we go get a Coke right now and talk about it?"

"Thanks," he said, "but I've got to get over to the sports clinic and put some time in there."

"What for?" Tara asked. "You're a finalist now. You don't need to worry about that anymore."

"Maybe not, but I can't be sure," he said. "It really wouldn't look very good if I quit now, and if they check, I want them to see the same public-spirited guy they saw Saturday night."

After a lightning-quick shower, Sean hopped into his Fiero and drove to the elementary school as fast as legally possible. It was the last place he felt like going. Not only was he tired and hungry, but he wasn't exactly jumping up and down about seeing Kate Harmon again. For one thing, she was sure to make a lot of remarks about how the Wolves had lost their last game to her school.

And if she knew that he'd made it into the final competition for Young Mr. Tarenton, she'd get in a few jabs about that, too.

But maybe she doesn't know I'm in the finals, he thought hopefully as he walked into the gym. After all, she's not interested in the contest, she thinks it's a total waste, so why should she bother to find out who the finalists are?

But the first voice he heard as he headed for his group of little gymnasts was Kate Harmon's. "Ta da!" she called out. "Here he is! It's the one, the only, Young Mr. Tarenton!"

To his embarrassment, Sean felt himself blushing. He wasn't sure why, since most of the kids hadn't paid any attention to Kate. It must have been Kate herself, standing there with her basketball, peering over her glasses at him with a smile on her lips and a gleam in her eyes. What was it about this girl, anyway? Why did he let her get his goat like this?

"Thanks," he said, coolly. "But I haven't won yet." Turning immediately to his group, he got them started on their warm-up exercises, and even though he was already limber, he exercised along with them. Behind him, he heard Kate bounce the basketball a couple of times. Go away, he thought, hoping she could read his mind. A few more days and we'll be out of each other's lives, so don't waste your time bugging me. Just go away.

Obviously, Kate couldn't read his mind, because the next thing Sean heard was her voice again, close by this time. "I didn't mean to em-

81

barrass you," she said. "Sometimes I don't know when to stop teasing." Whap went the basketball. "Of course," she went on, and Sean heard the smile in her voice, "if I really thought you couldn't take it, I'd stop. Shall I?"

Sean, in the middle of a sit-up, lay back on the floor and looked at her. That gleam in her eyes wasn't wicked, he noticed suddenly. It was just the gleam of somebody having a good time and inviting him to join in the fun. Without meaning to, he found himself laughing. "I can take it," he said.

"I thought you could," Kate said, laughing, too. "You're not so bad. I knew it all along." Bouncing the ball one last time, she raced across the floor and began organizing her group into teams.

Not so bad? Sean thought, shaking his head. Was that a compliment or a put-down? It was impossible to tell. In fact, Kate Harmon was impossible to figure out. With most girls, Sean knew where he stood. With Kate, he felt like he was walking a tightrope over a canyon. He'd made it across safely this time because he'd laughed instead of frowned. So just keep that up, Dubrow, he told himself, and maybe the time you put in here won't be so bad after all.

Feeling his energy return, Sean turned to his group and clapped his hands. "Today," he told them, "we're going to work on cartwheels. Can anybody do a cartwheel?"

Two hands were raised, and Sean watched as the kids did awkward, bent-leg attempts at cartwheels. "Not bad," he said, feeling generous, "but they can be better. Come on, let's get to work!"

For close to an hour, Sean worked with his group, trying to teach them how to do cartwheels. He didn't succeed, but he discovered that he'd had fun, anyway. Besides, he figured, it was better than writing an essay on why he should be Young Mr. Tarenton. Anything was better than writing an essay.

When Sean finally left the gym, he stepped outside into pouring rain. The early evening air was cool and the hard, steady rain made him shiver as he trotted toward his car. A hot shower, he thought, starting the engine, and then something to eat. Neither he nor his father was much of a cook, but Windy (short for Mrs. Windsor), their housekeeper, always left decent meals for them before she went home.

His stomach rumbling in anticipation, Sean nosed the car out of the parking lot and into the street. It was almost dark, and with the rain and the glare from the streetlights, he figured he'd better take it easy, no matter how hungry he was.

The steep hill leading toward the main street was slick with rain. Sean kept the car in second gear and turned his wipers up high. That's when he saw her. Even in the dark, even in the rain, there was no mistaking those long legs. A windbreaker flung over her head, Kate Harmon was hurrying down the wrong side of the road, trying to make the bus that had just pulled to a stop at the bottom of the hill.

One look at the bus, and Sean knew Kate didn't

have a chance of catching it. If it had been three or four days ago, he never would have stopped. But, now, even though she hadn't exactly been friendly, and even though he wasn't sure he even liked her, Sean couldn't drive on by. He knew how the buses ran in Tarenton — about every half hour, and usually not on time. If she had to stand in this rain for another thirty minutes, she'd be soaked to the bone. She might even get sick. That would get her off my back, he thought with a grin, but it would put her on my conscience.

Tapping lightly on the horn, Sean eased the car over to the side of the road. As Kate turned around to see who it was, the Fiero's headlights caught her full in the eyes, making her squint. Water dripping from her hair and face and rolling off her glasses, she trotted over and leaned down to the passenger window. As soon as she recognized Sean, she pulled the door open and slid inside.

"I take it you're offering me a ride," she said, shaking the raindrops from her hair, which was plastered to her head like a seal's. "Thanks. I wasn't looking forward to swimming home."

"Just point me in the right direction," Sean said, pulling back into the lane.

"Actually, it's kind of far from here." Kate shook her head again, giving Sean a light shower. "But in a car like this, I'll bet you could beat the bus to its next stop. Want to try?"

"Whatever you like," he told her, wishing she'd stop splattering him and his car with raindrops.

"Well, if you want to know what I'd really

84

like. . . ." Kate drew one wet sneaker onto the seat and grinned at him. "What I'd really like is a cheeseburger, some French fries, and a thick chocolate shake."

At the mention of food, Sean's stomach let out a rumble that could be heard over the Fiero's purring engine. Kate laughed, and without thinking, Sean laughed, too. Why not? he thought. I'm starving, and it won't hurt to spend a little time with her. Still laughing, he turned the car in the direction of Burger Benny's.

CHAPTER

9

"Okay," Kate said, sliding into the booth across from Sean, having called home. "My parents know where I am. They told me I should be home in an hour and you should be careful driving. It's still raining, and I'm still starving, so let's eat!"

Taking a big bite of her cheeseburger, Kate chewed silently for a minute, a satisfied expression on her face. Her hair, Sean noticed, had started to dry, and was quickly returning to its usual wild state. Her glasses were sliding down her nose, and the lighting did something to make her freckles stand out. Kate didn't seem to worry about how she looked, Sean thought with amazement. This kind of self-confidence was new to him.

"Boy," she said finally, finishing off some French fries, "I was really hungry."

"So I see," Sean remarked.

"Oh, sorry." Kate swallowed quickly and pushed a damp lock of hair off her forehead. "I've never been very good at making casual conversation."

"You don't seem to have any trouble at the sports clinic," Sean pointed out.

Instead of being insulted, Kate laughed, her eyes sparkling behind her water-spotted glasses. "You're right," she admitted. "I guess I feel more like I'm on my own turf there. Or at least that *you're* not on *your* turf." Glancing around at the other couples in the diner, many of whom were holding hands across the tables, she laughed again. "This is more your turf, isn't it?"

"Maybe," Sean said. "But I'm not a stranger to gyms, either. I'm a cheerleader, remember?"

"Oh, sure." Kate took off her glasses and wiped them on her sweat shirt. "In fact," she said, "I finally saw you perform."

"It was at Friday's game, right?" Sean asked quickly. "You were there, weren't you?"

Kate nodded, looking surprised. "You mean you saw me?"

"No. But I had a feeling you were there," Sean said, "cheering for St. Cloud."

"Well, sure I was," Kate admitted. "It's my school." She put her glasses back on and grinned again. "I bet you never expected us to win, did you?"

"That was a fluke," Sean told her. "The Wolves just had an off night."

"Maybe," she said doubtfully. "But anyway, *you* didn't have an off night."

87

"You mean you watched us?"

"You were pretty hard to miss," Kate joked. "No, really, I was curious. Like I said, I've never paid much attention to cheerleading, but since I knew you, I figured I might as well watch and see what it's all about." She stared at him for a second. "You're good," she told him. "The whole squad is good. I was impressed."

"I don't believe it," Sean said, pretending to be shocked. "You actually gave me a compliment!"

To his surprise, Kate blushed. She ducked her head so it was hard to tell, but it was definitely a blush.

"I guess you thought I couldn't stand you," she said, "because of the way I teased you about the Young Mr. Tarenton Contest."

"I got that impression, yes," Sean agreed.

"Then let's get the record straight. I can stand you." Still blushing, Kate looked at Sean quietly for a moment. Finally she said, "Why don't you tell me about the contest?"

Sean shook his head. "Come on, you're not interested in that."

"I am, too," Kate said. "I know I've teased you about it, and I can't promise I'll stop. After all, you asked for it, popping into the clinic just to get some good deeds on your record."

Sean started to protest, but Kate didn't give him a chance. "But just because I tease you doesn't mean I'm not interested. Besides, you may not like the clinic, but the kids don't know it. I've watched you, and they think you're some kind of god."

88

Once again, Sean started to say something, and once again, Kate didn't give him a chance. "Now don't puff up like a frog," she told him. "I said the *kids* think you're a god, not me. I know what you are."

"What's that?" Sean managed to ask.

"A sneaky guy," she said instantly. "But I like you, anyway. Now tell me about the contest."

Deciding that Kate wasn't as bad at conversation as she thought, Sean shrugged and told her about the competition Saturday night, expecting her to break in with a sarcastic comment every few seconds. But then he noticed that she had her chin in her hands and was listening, really listening, and he realized that she *was* interested. Describing his routine, he felt the excitement all over again. "It was like magic," he said. "Even if I'd tried to blow it, I don't think I could have. I've never been that good in my life."

Kate nodded. "My sister wants to be an actress," she said. "And she told me about this play she was in, in college. She had a big, emotional speech to give, and she said that while she gave it, she felt like she was floating, and the audience was floating with her."

"That's it!" Sean said excitedly. "I've read about people having the audience in the palm of their hands, and that's exactly what it feels like. Like no matter what you do, they're with you."

"Power," Kate said. "That's what it is. And while you've got it, you're on top of the world." Slurping up the last of her shake, she peered over her glasses at the clock above the cash register.

"Speaking of power, I don't have any. Not when it comes to getting home on time. We'd better go."

Looking down at his untouched fries, Sean felt a stab of disappointment. It was strange, because Kate Harmon was not the type of girl he usually spent time with. She wasn't beautiful, for one thing. Plus she didn't seem to have a terrifically high opinion of him. She could stand him, that's what she'd said, and Sean liked girls who could do more than stand him. Still, he realized that he didn't want to leave yet.

But Kate was already putting on her coat, fishing around in the pockets for money. Pulling out a wrinkled five-dollar bill, she slapped it on the table. "Want to make a bet?"

"About what?"

"About the Tarenton Wolves," she said. "I'm willing to bet the change I have coming to me that that game they lost to St. Cloud wasn't just a fluke."

Sean laughed. "You'll lose."

"Maybe." Kate laughed, too. "But I don't have much change coming, so why not?"

"You're on." Sean stuck out his hand and they shook across the table. It was a quick shake, but long enough for him to notice that her hand was warm and slender and strong. It seemed to fit his perfectly.

As they left the diner, Kate noticed a bus approaching at the other end of the block. "I think I'll take it," she said, changing directions. "It's not that I don't like your car, but I really do live kind of far out, and I'm sure you've got stuff to do." Without waiting for an answer, she flashed Sean a quick smile, drew her jacket over her head, and dashed across the street just in time to catch the bus.

Driving home alone, Sean tried to think about the essay he had to write for the contest. Instead, he found himself thinking about Kate Harmon's sparkling grin, her long legs, and the way her warm hand had felt in his.

"Sean!" Tara tried not to sound annoyed, but she couldn't help it. She'd been wanting to talk to him all during cheerleading practice, but he'd acted as if he was in another world, barely noticing that she or anyone else existed. So she'd planted herself outside the boys' locker room, knowing he couldn't miss seeing her there. But he still had that faraway, glazed look in his eyes, and she practically had to yell to get his attention. "Sean!"

"Oh. Tara. Hi." Still breathing hard from the workout Coach Engborg had put them through, Sean turned, his hand on the locker room door. "What's up?"

Hot and tired herself, Tara waved a hand in front of his face, trying to bring his mind back to the present. "Where are you, anyway?" she asked. "Are you sure you're still on the same planet with the rest of us?"

Instead of laughing, Sean looked confused, which made her even more annoyed. "Sean! Wake up!"

Giving his head a quick shake as if trying to

clear the cobwebs out of it, Sean finally smiled. "Sorry," he said. "Got something on my mind."

"That's obvious," Tara remarked. "I hope it's the essay."

"Essay?"

"You know, the essay for the contest," Tara reminded him. "The Young Mr. Tarenton Contest, remember? Hawaii? Sand? Palm trees?"

"Don't worry; I remember," Sean said with a laugh.

"Well? Did you write the essay?"

"No, not yet."

"But, Sean, it's got to be in in a couple of days!" Hearing how pushy she sounded, Tara took a deep breath and forced herself to smile. Being bossy wouldn't get her anywhere with Sean — certainly not to Hawaii. "I just wanted you to know," she said sweetly, "that if you have any trouble with it, I'll be glad to help. In fact, I already have some ideas."

"Great," he said. "I'd like to hear them, but not right now, okay? I've got to get something worked out, and then I'll give you a call. Or I'll talk to you tomorrow, maybe." Shaking his head again, Sean gave her a distracted grin and pushed open the locker room door, leaving Tara standing in the hallway wondering what could possibly be so important that it would push the contest right out of his mind.

Driving to the elementary school, Sean was wondering the same thing. He knew what had kept him from concentrating on that essay, of course, but he just couldn't believe it. Kate Harmon? It didn't make any sense. She wasn't his type. If anybody was his type, Tara was. And it wasn't just the difference in looks, either. He understood girls like Tara. They played the same kind of game he did, keeping boys wondering, never really letting any one of them get too close because it was much more fun that way. But as far as Sean could tell, the only game Kate Harmon played was basketball. She was so open, so up-front, there was absolutely no mystery about her.

Except, Sean thought as he went into the gym, the mystery of why he couldn't stop thinking about her. Why, every time he'd tried to write a sentence of that essay last night, he'd found himself writing her name, just like a kid in grade school. Or why, whenever he tried to picture himself in Hawaii, he saw images of Kate instead, leaping around the gym, wolfing down her cheeseburger, sitting across the booth from him with her chin in her hands and that mischievous, intelligent gleam in her eyes.

And the thing that made the least sense of all was that when Sean had finished helping his group stumble through some more cartwheels, he found himself waiting by the gym door, waiting for Kate to come out.

"Hi," she said, looking surprised. "I saw you rush out of the gym, and I figured you'd already zipped off in that flashy red car of yours."

"I thought maybe we could both zip off in it," Sean told her, hoping he sounded like he didn't much care one way or the other — which he did.

"I'm always thirsty after I get out of here, so I was thinking of stopping for a Coke. Want to come?"

"I don't know." Kate hitched her canvas bag higher on her shoulder and looked at her watch. "I've got a ton of homework."

"So do I," Sean said, "but I always do a better job if I'm not thirsty."

Kate laughed. "Me, too," she said. "Okay, let's go."

Sean meant to take her back to Burger Benny's, or to the Pizza Palace, but as he drove, he realized that he didn't really want to go some place crowded and noisy. Maybe in a quiet place he could figure out what it was about Kate that got under his skin. And once he figured that out, he could forget about her.

The road to the lake was coming up on the left, and Sean glanced over at Kate. "Feel like feeding the ducks?"

"No bread crumbs," she said. Then she laughed. "But they're too fat anyway, and I love the lake. So let's go."

The ducks greeted them noisily as Sean and Kate walked down to the bank, but the minute they discovered the two were empty-handed, the birds waddled away, squawking insults. It was late afternoon and the sun was on its way down, its last rays shimmering across the dark water. Except for Sean and Kate, no one else was there.

Kate immediately picked up some stones and started skipping them across the surface of the lake. "This is great," she said. "Don't you wish we didn't have homework? We could stay here for hours."

Sean nodded. "What I have to do isn't really homework, though. I've got to write an essay for that contest about why I should be chosen Young Mr. Tarenton."

Kate pushed her glasses up and grinned. "What are you going to say?"

"I don't know. I guess just some stuff about how I'm a good student and a good cheerleader."

"And a volunteer at the sports clinic — don't forget that," Kate pointed out. She flung another stone across the water and shook her head. "Sorry. I couldn't resist it."

Sean wasn't really insulted. He'd been expecting it, and besides, she was right. He'd volunteered at the clinic for only one reason: because it would look good. "Maybe I should just tell them the truth," he said, "that they should make me Young Mr. Tarenton because I want to go to Hawaii."

Kate laughed. "You could try it," she said, "but I have a feeling it won't get you very far."

"Maybe not," Sean agreed. "But it doesn't really matter."

"It doesn't?" Kate raised her eyebrows. "It doesn't, really?"

"Not as much as it used to." Sean was surprised to hear himself say it, but he realized it was true. Not that he didn't want to go to Hawaii, of course. But for some reason, he wasn't feeling quite as excited about it.

Sean looked at Kate, her short hair ruffling in

the breeze, and he suddenly realized that she was the reason. He'd gone to the sports clinic because he thought it was his ticket to Hawaii, and he'd found somebody who drove Hawaii out of his mind. It was hard to believe, but it was true.

Picking up a stone himself, Sean drew his arm back and, with a flick of his wrist, sent it skipping across the lake.

"That's it!" Kate cried. "That's why you should be Young Mr. Tarenton! I mean, who else can skip a rock four times before it sinks?"

She was laughing, her glasses once more half-way down her nose, and before she could push them up, Sean moved to her side and pushed them up for her. Instead of taking his hand away, he brushed it gently over the freckles on her cheek, and slid it around her neck. He still wasn't sure what it was about Kate Harmon that got under his skin, but as he bent to kiss her, he realized he liked having her there, and that was all that mattered.

CHAPTER

10

"Hey, Garrison,
Hear that roar?
It's the Tarenton Wolves
Howling at your door!
Better open up,
Better let 'em in,
'Cause the Tarenton Wolves
Are sure to win!"

It was a close game, the kind that Hope usually enjoyed best of all. There was nothing like a crowd that was alive and on its feet to make her do her best.

Today, though, Hope barely heard the crowd. She tried to concentrate on her moves, but every time she came close to Peter — which during this cheer was much too often — she felt her smile disappear and her body get stiff. Coach Engborg is going to notice for sure, she thought, as she whirled her way across the floor. Peter was waiting, as he was supposed to, to give her a push that would send her spinning back to the center to join Tara. Just pretend he's a stranger, she told herself. Or pretend he's a friend. Pretend anything, just as long as it makes you forget what he really is.

It didn't work, of course. There was still too much anger between Peter and Hope for either one of them to pretend it didn't exist. And as Hope got closer to him, her face tightened and she felt the urge to run in the opposite direction.

Watching her, Peter's own smile disappeared. If he hadn't had to keep an eye on her, he would have looked the other way. Instead, he stared into the space above her head.

It was a simple move. When Hope got to him, he was supposed to take her hand, twirl her around, and appear to give her a push, making her spin back away from him. Hope was the one doing all the work, and the push was supposed to be a fake.

This time, though, it wasn't a fake. Not that Peter would have deliberately shoved her, no matter how he felt. But somehow, when he spun her away from him, he realized that he'd spun her a little too hard. Instead of twirling gracefully toward Tara, Hope stumbled right into her.

Only Tara seemed to notice; the other cheerleaders were too busy performing the routine. And as mistakes went, it was a small one. Hope recovered immediately, and went right on as if nothing had happened. But something *had* happened, and neither she nor Peter could forget about it.

That had been the halftime cheer, and now the squad had a few minutes to get some water and catch their breath before the game resumed. They spent those few minutes in their waiting room, the narrow hall between their two locker rooms, where they could keep an eye on the wall clock. They usually exchanged jokes or discussed a routine or complained about homework. Tonight, though, as Olivia was describing the incredibly long research paper she'd just been assigned in social studies, she caught Hope's eye and stopped in the middle of a sentence.

Hope wasn't looking at her, and Olivia was grateful. Because Hope — shy, quiet, calm Hope — was obviously furious, her dark eyes flashing and her mouth a straight, tight line across her face. She was staring at Peter, and before Olivia could say anything, Peter walked across the room and stood in front of Hope.

"Sorry about that push," he said, crushing a paper cup and dropping it in the wastebasket. "I guess my timing was a little off."

He doesn't sound sorry at all, Olivia thought, wondering what he was talking about. She started to ask, but before she could, Hope spoke.

"I don't think your timing was off at all," Hope said, and her voice was cold. "So please don't apologize."

Peter had started to walk away, but now he stopped. "What do you mean?" he asked.

"You know what I mean," Hope said. "You did that on purpose. If you hadn't pushed me, I never would have bumped into Tara, and it didn't have anything to do with timing."

By now, Jessica, Sean, and Tara had stopped talking, and everyone was completely quiet.

"I can't believe you think that," Peter said quietly. "Be as mad at me as you like, but don't accuse me of something that isn't true."

"No fights allowed on school grounds," Sean joked, trying to lighten things up. "You can get suspended for that, remember?"

Tara punched him in the arm. "Not funny," she whispered.

Neither Hope nor Peter paid any attention to the interruption. They just kept staring at each other as if they were the only people in the hall. Finally, Hope spoke again.

"I think I'll wait in the locker room," she said, never taking her eyes off Peter. "It's too crowded here."

Peter watched her go, and then looked around, a blush spreading over his face as he realized he'd had an audience. Frowning, he headed for the boys' locker room. "Bang on the door when it's time, will you?" he said to Sean as he went.

"Whew!" Sean wiped his forehead and leaned against the wall, pretending to be weak with relief. "That was too close for comfort! I actually thought I might have to referee."

"Don't be ridiculous," Jessica told him. "Besides, it's not funny."

"You're right," Olivia agreed. "It's not funny.

It's weird. I never thought I'd ever see Hope Chang angry. Or Peter, either. They're both so . . . I don't know, so controlled. Especially Hope."

"Hope was controlled," Sean pointed out. "That was controlled fury you saw."

"What's it all about, anyway?" Tara asked.

"It has to be the contest," Olivia said. "It started when Peter dropped out. I've been meaning to talk to Hope about it, but I just haven't."

"Better wait," Sean advised with a grin. "She may be controlled now, but you never know when she might explode."

"Maybe you could talk to Peter," Jessica suggested to him. "They may be mad at each other, but they're also miserable. Which means they don't like being mad at each other."

"Sure, I'll give it a shot," Sean agreed. Since he'd kissed Kate, he was feeling the opposite of miserable. Maybe some of it would rub off on Peter. "I'll talk to him right after the game."

"And I'll talk to Hope." Olivia eyed the big clock on the wall. Halftime was over. "Come on. And keep your fingers crossed that they don't start an argument in the middle of a cheer," she said, and she was only half joking.

But Peter and Hope must have given themselves a talking-to, because even though they still avoided each other's eyes, and even though their smiles were strained, they performed their routines flawlessly.

There *was* a fight, but not between the two cheerleaders. Instead, it broke out between the two teams. With a minute to go, the score was

101

tied, and when a Garrison player jostled Bill Hadley, Bill immediately shouted, "Foul!" The other player disagreed, and with the game so close and the tension so high, the two got into a shoving match. A referee broke it up, and then Garrison scored, pulling ahead by two points, which was how the game ended.

"Not fair," Sean said, as he and Peter went into the locker room. "That was a foul, and the Wolves should have gotten a free throw."

"Mmm." Peter was changing his clothes as quickly as possible. He could shower at home; all he wanted now was to get out.

"But we're still the best, so I guess it doesn't really matter," Sean said.

"Mmm."

"The fight was kind of exciting, though, huh?"

"Mmm."

Sean grinned. "Almost as exciting as the one at halftime."

Finally, Peter paid attention. "Halftime? There was a fight at halftime?"

"How could you miss it?" Sean asked. "You were in it."

"Oh." Peter felt himself blushing again, and turned to his locker, pretending to look for something inside. "*That* fight."

"Right." Sean pulled on a pair of socks and then stared at Peter's back. He and Peter weren't close friends, and he felt a little awkward in this situation. But still, he liked the guy. "Want to talk about it?"

"There's not much to talk about," Peter said

with a sigh. Turning around, he flopped back on the bench and crossed his arms over his eyes. "Hope's mad because I quit the contest, and I'm mad because she asked me to enter it in the first place." He sighed again. "It seems like a stalemate to me."

"Come on, I don't buy that," Sean said.

Peter raised an arm and peered at Sean. "So what's your solution?"

"Oh. Well." Sean didn't have one. "Give me some time to think about it."

"I've got plenty of that," Peter told him.

Sean thought, but he couldn't come up with anything. "Listen," he said finally, "Hope's mad because you quit, and you're mad because you entered. So you're even, right?"

"Right," Peter agreed. "We're evenly mad."

"So forget it," Sean said.

"Forget it?" Peter took both arms off his face this time. "That's your solution?"

"Why not? Makes sense to me."

"It would," Peter said dryly. "But I don't think you understand what it's like to . . . to care about somebody so much, and then to have something like this happen."

"I wouldn't be so sure about that," Sean told him, thinking of Kate. "But even if that were true, I still think you should forget it — if you still care about her, that is."

Peter was silent.

"Otherwise," Sean went on, "it sounds to me like you're just being stubborn."

"Stubborn?" Peter sat up. "Don't talk to me

103

about being stubborn! If you want to know what stubborn is, talk to Hope!"

Over in the girls' locker room, Olivia was just discovering what Peter meant. She'd deliberately waited until Tara and Jessica had gone, expecting that Hope would be glad to talk about the whole thing. After all, Hope had come to her before when she'd been bothered by something. But when she brought up the subject, Hope immediately tried to change it. Of course, Olivia had always known that Hope had a strong will. In fact, she'd always admired it. But this wasn't a strong will she was trying to talk to. This was stubbornness, pure and simple.

"Olivia," Hope said, brushing her dark hair until it crackled, "I know you care. Otherwise you wouldn't be trying to talk to me about this."

"Good," Olivia said. "Now that we've got that out of the way, let's — "

"What you don't understand is that I don't want to talk about it," Hope interrupted smoothly.

"But Hope!" Olivia couldn't believe it. "You're obviously unhappy. And so's Peter. Maybe I can help."

Hope shook her head, and started putting on some lipstick.

Olivia decided to ignore the gesture. "I don't mean I can fix things between you two. But it's not a good idea to keep everything bottled up, you know. And if you talk, maybe you'll find out you're not so mad anymore. Then, maybe things'll work out by themselves."

Hope put her lipstick away and reached for her jacket. She didn't answer.

What am I doing this for? Olivia wondered. It's like talking to a brick wall. Maybe they can work things out, and maybe they can't. And maybe the whole thing's just none of my business. "Okay," she said. "I won't bring it up again, Hope. But you're my friend, so if you ever *do* want to talk about it, let me know."

"Thank you, Livvy." Hope smiled finally, a genuine smile. "I'm sorry if I was rude. And I'll remember what you said."

When Hope got home, the house was quiet, and she let out a sigh of relief. Her father must have had to work late, and her mother and little brother were probably in the den. So far, she'd managed to keep her fight with Peter a secret from her parents, and she wanted things to stay that way. It had been bad enough keeping quiet in front of Olivia, but it would be worse with her parents. In fact, it would be impossible. She'd have to talk about it if they asked, and as far as she was concerned, there was nothing to talk about. Besides, she might cry, and she hated crying. It was hard sometimes, holding everything in. But it was better than blubbering like a baby.

Slipping off her jacket, Hope walked into the kitchen and poured herself some orange juice. She was still upset, and what she wanted most was to get to her room without having to smile at another living soul.

"Hope?" Caroline Chang stood in the kitchen

doorway. She had a soft green bathrobe on, and she looked a little groggy. "I'm embarrassed — I actually fell asleep watching television." She laughed and poured herself some water. "How was the game?"

"It was exciting," Hope said, "but Tarenton lost."

"Oh, that's too bad."

"But we're still in first place."

"That's good." Hope's mother drank some water and put her glass in the dishwasher. "And how is Peter?"

Hope put her own glass in the dishwasher, letting her hair fall over her face to hide the expression on it. "He's well."

"Well?" Mrs. Chang laughed again. "That sounds so formal!"

"I mean, he's fine. I think." Straightening up, Hope started for the door, but her mother's words stopped her.

"Hope? Your father and I couldn't help noticing that Peter hasn't been by lately. Is anything wrong?"

Hope nodded, wishing she could just come right out and say she didn't want to talk about it. "I'm afraid so, Mother."

"What happened?"

"We've had an argument." Taking a deep breath, Hope told her mother about Peter dropping out of the contest and about how they hadn't spoken to each other since. She was careful to give Peter's side of it, even though she didn't think it was worth two cents, because if she hadn't her mother would have insisted on hearing it. Her parents had always told her there were two sides to any argument, and it was true. The problem was, Peter was on the wrong side this time. But she didn't say that.

"I can understand why you're disappointed," Mrs. Chang said, when Hope had finished. "But maybe it was too much to ask of Peter."

"He should have said so in the first place," Hope said. "That's why I'm angry."

"Are you sure he didn't try to tell you?"

"Of course I'm sure," Hope told her. "I *did* want to go to Hawaii, but if Peter didn't want to be in that contest, he could have told me. He's got a mind of his own."

"Yes," her mother agreed, "but people are always doing things they don't much like in order to please other people. Maybe that's what Peter was trying to do — please you."

"He would have pleased me more by being honest," Hope said. Raising her chin, she smiled. "Mother, will you excuse me, please? I have homework to do."

CHAPTER

"Is this really my son I see before me?" Mark Dubrow, a handsome, older version of Sean, peered around the doorway, his dark eyebrows raised skeptically. "It's only nine o'clock at night and you're in your bedroom studying?"

Laughing, Sean threw down his essay and stretched until he was more comfortable on the bed. "Well, I'm a little tired after that game tonight," he said. "Besides, I've got to get this essay done or I might as well kiss Hawaii good-bye."

Sean's father came over, picked up the notebook Sean had been writing in, and read aloud. " 'I believe that I would make a good Young Mr. Tarenton because. . . .' " He turned the paper over, then looked at Sean. "That's it?"

"Well, I'm not finished yet," Sean said. Then he laughed again. "Who am I kidding? I haven't even started."

"Something else on your mind?" his father asked.

"There sure is," Sean told him, a grin spreading across his face. "A girl, to be exact."

"No wonder you can't work." His father laughed. "So why aren't you out with her right now? I know it's a school night, but you had time to get a Coke, didn't you?"

"I did," Sean said, "but she didn't." He'd called Kate after the game, as soon as he'd finished talking to Peter, but she was up to her ears in a paper on Emily Dickinson. "I'd rather be with you," she'd said, "but I don't think my teacher would accept you as a very good excuse for not turning this paper in on time. Anyway, I'll see you at the sports clinic tomorrow, won't I?"

That was true, and Sean couldn't wait to get there. But it seemed like such a long time between now and then. Boy, Dubrow, he told himself, you've got it bad.

"Well?" His father was waiting, his eyebrows still raised. "What's she like? She must really be something to make you so distracted you can't concentrate on Hawaii."

"She is," Sean agreed. Shoving another pillow behind his head, he pushed himself up against the headboard. "She's different from most girls — I mean, most of the girls I usually go out with."

"What do you mean?"

"Oh, you know, Dad. I usually go for what's on the outside, not what's on the inside. I don't mean that Kate — that's her name, Kate — isn't pretty. She is . . . well sort of . . . and she's got legs that don't stop. But the way she looks isn't the first thing you notice about her." He laughed, remembering. "In fact, the first thing I noticed about her was her mouth. She tends to say exactly what she thinks."

"Nothing wrong with that," his father said.

"No. I don't mind it now," Sean told him. "I guess what I'm saying is that she's not my usual type."

His father gave a low whistle. "This sounds serious."

"Why do you say that?"

"Well, your mother wasn't my type, either," Mark Dubrow said, his voice softening. "But she was the one I married, and I never regretted it." He held up his hand. "I know, I know. Marriage isn't on your mind. All I meant was that your type may not be what's going to make you happy. And you sure look happy now, so I must be right." He headed for the door, chuckling.

After his father left, Sean picked up his notebook again, but he still couldn't come up with anything original to write. Think, he ordered himself. Think about Hawaii. Think about the sand and the water and the starry nights.

Instead, he thought about Kate. And instead of writing about why he should be Young Mr. Tarenton, he found himself making a list of people to invite to a party. After all, he was in love, and he wanted everyone to meet the girl he was in love with. What better way than at a party?

"Oh, no!" Kate said, when Sean told her about it. "I'm going to feel like I'm on display."

"No, you won't," Sean argued. "Besides, most

of them are my friends. You'll like them. And they'll like you."

It was Thursday afternoon and the two of them were at the lake again. Kate wasn't allowed to go out on school nights, and even though Sean was disappointed, he figured it was just as well. The deadline for his essay was tomorrow, and if he didn't write it tonight, he'd be in big trouble. Even though Hawaii didn't excite him as much as Kate, he wasn't the kind of guy to turn his back on a free trip. He'd come this far, so he might as well go all the way.

"I'm sure I'll like them," Kate said. "That's not what I'm worried about. Just don't make a big deal about introducing me, okay? I get flustered when everybody stares. I guess I should dress nice, huh?"

Sean looked at her faded jeans, stretched-out sweat shirt, and scuffed sneakers. He suddenly realized that he'd never seen her in anything else, and he also realized that he didn't care. "Don't change a thing," he said, pulling her to him. "Just be yourself."

Sean had scheduled his party for Saturday night, after the game with Hillsborough, one of Tarenton High's easiest rivals. It was another close score, but this time the Wolves came out on top, and the party turned out to be a victory celebration.

"This is great," Patrick said to Jessica, as they helped themselves to slices from the eight-foot-long hero sandwich on the Dubrows' dining room

111

table. "There's nothing like a party after a win."

"I know," Jessica agreed. "And just wait until the Wolves take the championship. Then you'll really see some celebrating."

"It's too early to start cheering for that," David commented, reaching for the pickles. "Not that I don't think they'll win, but they're only ahead by three games, you know."

"It's enough," Olivia argued. "My gosh, they play dozens of games. They can't be expected to win every last one of them."

"True," David said. "But they do have to win more than anybody else."

"They will," Olivia said confidently. "The Wolves are the best. And remember, they've got the best cheerleading squad behind them."

"Your modesty is overwhelming," David joked, stealing some chips from her plate. "Tell me, though, was it my imagination or did I see a little stumble in one of your routines tonight?"

Olivia blushed. She *had* stumbled, which was very unusual, especially since it was during one of their easiest cheers.

"Don't pick on our captain," Tara told David. "After all, she cheers as much as the Wolves play, so she can't be expected to be perfect every time, either."

"That's not what Coach Engborg would say." Olivia laughed. "But thanks, anyway, Tara. My mind was somewhere else, I guess. I think I was worried that Peter would refuse to take Hope's hand during that cheer, or that she wouldn't let him." She sighed. "I guess you guys noticed that Hope isn't here tonight."

"Peter came, though," Jessica said, and they all looked over at their fellow cheerleader. He was sitting glumly in the living room, ignoring the laughter and conversation going on around him.

Peter had agreed to come, not because he was really in the mood for a party, but because he thought it might take his mind off Hope. After all, if things were over between them, he should get out and circulate, shouldn't he? Not that he was looking for another girl — it would be a long time before he did that — but still, anything was better than sitting at home, brooding, and hoping his mother didn't start asking him what was wrong.

Of course, he realized, all he was doing was brooding here, instead of at home. Snap out of it, Rayman, he told himself. Either snap out of it or go home. Sean didn't throw this party so you could come and spoil it.

Forcing a pleasant, interested expression on his face, Peter sat up straighter and looked around for someone to talk to. Unfortunately, the first person he saw was Diana Tucker, who had just come in with Bill Hadley. Diana looked beautiful, as usual, with her blonde hair, golden California skin, and her perfect clothes.

But seeing her only made Peter think of Hope again. A while back, he'd almost fallen for Diana. What a sucker he'd been! She'd only pretended to be interested in him so she could weasel her way onto the squad. It hadn't worked, but Peter still couldn't believe how close he'd come to giving up Hope for someone like that. Slumping back into the leather cushions of the couch, he wondered grumpily why Sean had invited her at all.

Tara, taking a second slice of hero, was wondering the same thing. Diana was the last person on earth she wanted to see at that moment. And Bill Hadley was the next to the last. They reminded her of the contest, which Diana obviously thought Bill should have won, even though he didn't even make the finals; and they also reminded her that Sean hadn't shown her his essay yet. That wasn't a good sign. Sean was the first to admit that he didn't write award-winning papers, and since Tara was better at it, she'd expected him to ask her for help. She thought they were in this together, but the way Sean had been acting the last few days, she was beginning to get worried.

"Where is Sean, anyway?" she asked.

"The last time I saw our host, he was looking out the front door," David said. "He must be expecting someone special, because he's been waiting by that door since the party started."

As David said, Sean was waiting by the front door. He'd had plenty of girls over to his house since he'd started dating, but Kate was the first one he'd ever waited for like this — like a kid waiting for Christmas morning. Kate hadn't been able to make the game, so her mother was driving her over, and Sean kept checking his watch every two minutes, wondering what was taking her so long. Had she gotten sick? Had she had a flat tire? Had she decided not to come?

He checked his watch again, then laughed at himself. The party had started exactly twenty minutes ago. Kate wasn't even late yet, so why was he propping open the door like this? You've really got it bad, he told himself for the hundredth time.

It was true, though, he *did* have it bad, so bad that he didn't even care that Bill and Diana were here. He'd stuck his head in the locker room after the game, inviting some of the team, and Bill Hadley had been there with them. Sean didn't have much use for the guy, even if he was a good basketball player, but tonight he didn't care. Tonight, he felt good about the whole world.

Just then, he heard the crunch of tires on the driveway, and saw headlights flashing across the front window. Pulling open the door, he looked out into the cool night.

"See you later!" Kate's voice called out. "Sean said he'd drive me home, so don't worry!"

A car door slammed, and then Kate was there, striding along the curved stone path toward the front door, the porch light glinting on her glasses.

"Hi!" she said, as Sean stepped outside to meet her. "I'm not late, am I? I just finished typing that stupid paper fifteen minutes ago. Homework on a Saturday night, I can't believe it! But since we're going out tomorrow, I knew I'd better get it done or I'd be in big trouble."

Sean barely heard what she was saying. He

was too busy watching her, admiring the way her long legs moved, and noticing that she wasn't wearing her usual sports clinic get-up. Instead, she had on a soft swirling skirt and a rust-colored sweater that changed her hair from plain to reddish brown. He reached out a hand, felt her strong fingers grip his, and pulled her tight against him.

"Let's forget the party," he whispered, kissing her freckled cheek. "Nobody will miss us, and right now I don't feel like sharing you with anybody."

"Oh, no," she said laughing. "I've been slaving away all night and I'm ready for a party. Besides, you're the host. You've got responsibilities."

But when he pulled her to him, ten minutes passed before they went inside the house.

"Well, Tara," Diana said, "where's Sean? I expected you to be right by his side, and I haven't seen him since I came in."

"He must be in the kitchen," Tara said, wishing Diana would quietly disappear. "This is his party, after all, so he's in charge. I'm just a guest, like you. And I'm not his date."

"Oh?" Diana's blue eyes widened in fake surprise. "I didn't think you'd let him out of your sight for a minute."

Tara sighed and put her paper plate down. There was nothing like this California girl to ruin the appetite. "What are you talking about, Diana?"

"Well, I just mean that since he's your ticket to Hawaii, I thought you might be a little worried.

You know Sean. He does like to play around, and if you're not careful, he might decide to take somebody else." With a toss of her head, she flung her blonde hair back and gave Tara a small smile. "Of course, he has to *win* first, and since that's not going to happen, maybe it doesn't matter."

Tara decided not to say anything. If she ignored her, Diana just might take the hint and go away.

But if Diana understood the hint, she refused to acknowledge it. "By the way," she went on, "I couldn't help noticing that the famous Varsity Cheerleading Squad has been having a little trouble lately. I've seen a few bumps and stumbles in the last few games, and if I've seen them, you can be sure Ardith Engborg has seen them."

Tara bit her lip, but she couldn't keep herself from rising to the bait. "We're not perfect, Diana," she said. "But we're the best, and our *coach* knows that. Besides, I don't think you should be talking to me about our mistakes. You should be talking to Bill Hadley about the team's mistakes. The Wolves are only three games ahead of Deep River, you know, and if they don't shape up, they could lose the championship."

Tara didn't really believe that the Wolves would lose, but it made her feel good to see Diana frown when she said it. There, she thought, now maybe she'll find somebody else to bother.

But Diana recovered quickly. "The Wolves are the best basketball team in the state," she said coolly, "and if they lose, it might just be because they had such a bumbling cheerleading squad backing them up." Tossing her hair again, she walked away, leaving Tara by herself at last.

Her appetite completely ruined, Tara decided to find somebody to dance with. So far, all she'd done was worry about Sean and get insulted by Diana, and that was a waste of a good party.

Turning from the table, she headed into the living room, where most of the kids were gathered. Someone had just slipped a cassette into the tape deck, and as the rock music pounded out, Tara glanced around for a partner. That's when she finally saw Sean.

He was standing in the doorway of the living room, a big smile on his face and a tall girl by his side. Tara looked at the girl closely. She had fine brown hair whose curls were turning to frizz; nice but unmade-up brown eyes behind a pair of glasses; and beautiful, pale skin sprinkled with freckles. She was laughing, which made her look pretty, and from what Tara could see, she had the long, lean figure of an athlete.

She wasn't Sean's type; Tara knew that. But Sean didn't seem to know or care. He was looking at the girl, laughing with her, and even though Tara had seen him happy before, she'd never seen him like this.

"Hey, everybody!" Sean called out, his arm around the girl's waist. "This is Kate!"

Tara's stomach felt heavy, as if she'd just swallowed a rock. Diana was right about one thing, she thought. Sean had found somebody else, and from the way he looks tonight, you might as well put away your bikini.

CHAPTER

12

After a workout like the one Ardith Engborg put them through on the Monday after Sean's party, the cheerleaders were usually too tired to talk. The coach, as everyone expected and as Diana had predicted, had not missed a single one of their stumbles. True, the mistakes had been small ones, and, as Tara said, the squad wasn't perfect. Nobody knew that better than Coach Engborg, but she also knew that little mistakes led to big ones, and if she didn't do something about it, her near-perfect squad would really start to slip.

"I'm not sure what the problem is," she'd said as the squad gathered in the gym for practice. Actually, she *did* know, or sensed, that there was trouble between Hope and Peter. The two of them were obviously avoiding each other, and whenever they had to come together during a routine, they were like opposite poles of a magnet, their anger forcing them apart. But Hope and Peter weren't the only ones. Everyone on the squad — even Jessica, the perfectionist, and Olivia, the veteran — was making little mistakes in timing or placement. Sean had enough energy for five cheerleaders, but his exuberance was making him sloppy. Tara was the only one who hadn't goofed lately, but good as she was, Tara couldn't hold the squad together by herself.

Coach Engborg wasn't overly worried, but she did want to nip this thing in the bud. "I don't know what the problem is," she'd repeated, "but I do know the solution: work."

So for over an hour, the coach worked the squad, pushing them toward that perfection she knew was just out of their reach. When she finally let them go, she still wasn't satisfied, but she wasn't ready to give up, either. "There's a game tomorrow, as I'm sure you know," she told them, watching them head toward the locker rooms. "And by tomorrow, I want to see some improvement."

Instead of feeling wiped out to the point of total silence, the girls were still bubbling over with talk about Kate Harmon. None of them liked gossip, but this wasn't really gossip, and besides, seeing Sean head over heels in love was such a strange phenomenon that they had to discuss it or burst.

"Did you see the way he looked at her?" Olivia asked, as they got dressed. "It was like he'd never seen a girl before."

"I think he's as amazed as we are," Jessica

said. "The big playboy, Sean Dubrow, finally found somebody to worship besides himself."

"And he really is crazy about her," Olivia agreed. "I can see why, too."

"Why?" Hope asked, too curious to ignore the talk. "Is she beautiful?"

"No . . . she's not," Jessica said thoughtfully. "But I don't think that's what Sean cares about, which is why I can tell he's serious."

"She's funny," Olivia told Hope. "And she's smart. And," she said with a grin, "she doesn't give two hoots about Sean's ego."

"And Sean doesn't care?" Hope asked.

"Nope." Olivia laughed. "It's not that she puts him down or anything. It's obvious that she's crazy about him, too. She's just very honest and she says what she thinks. And if what she's thinking isn't complimentary to Sean, she says it anyway. But not to be mean. She actually makes him laugh at himself. I really like her."

"So do I," Jessica said.

And so does Sean, Tara thought, slipping out of the locker room. And if she had to be perfectly honest with herself, so did she. Kate Harmon was a little too outspoken, as far as Tara was concerned, but that was a minor fault. She was a very friendly, very nice girl, and try as Tara might, she couldn't find anything about her to dislike.

At first, Tara had decided that she really *should* put away her bikini. If Sean won that contest, it wouldn't be Tara he'd share his ticket with. It would be Kate.

But the more she talked to Kate, the more she decided that maybe she still had a chance. Kate might want to go, but her parents would never let her. Not with a boy, not even if a chaperone went along. "I'm the baby of the family," she'd said. "It has its privileges, but flying to Hawaii with your boyfriend isn't one of them. Besides," she'd said, laughing and pointing to her face, "see these freckles? These freckles mean I burn. What's the point of an oceanside vacation if I have to stay out of the sun?"

Tara had been on the verge of mentioning sunscreens that would solve the problem, but she'd changed her mind. Kate didn't seem all that interested in Hawaii, anyway. And since she couldn't go, and Tara could, why should Tara give up? All she had to do now was make sure *Sean* didn't give up.

Wednesday's game was away, at Garrison, and instead of using her own car, Tara rode with Sean. Usually, she wouldn't have passed up a chance to drive, but this time she had too many important things to say. For a moment, it looked like Hope was going to ride with them, but at the last minute, Hope changed her mind, and Tara was able to be alone with Sean.

"Listen," she said, as soon as they pulled out of the parking lot, "we've got to talk."

"Talk away," Sean told her. "I can listen and drive at the same time."

"I'm not worried about that," Tara said. "What I'm worried about is the contest."

"Why?"

"Why?" Tara shook her head. "I can't believe you don't know why!"

Turning to her, Sean smiled and shrugged. "Do I have to guess or are you going to tell me?"

"I'll tell you," Tara sighed. Reaching into her canvas bag, she pulled out a copy of Sean's essay, which he'd given to her the night of his party. "It's this," she said, stabbing at the paper with her finger. "This is why I'm worried."

"My essay?" Sean asked. "Why? What's wrong with it?"

"*Wrong* with it?" Clearing her throat, Tara began to read. " 'I believe that I should be elected Young Mr. Tarenton because I am young, I'm from Tarenton, and I'm a boy.' " Stopping, she gave Sean a fierce look from her green eyes.

Sean laughed. "I was just trying for a little humor, see? I could hardly be Young Ms. Tarenton, could I?"

"It's not funny," Tara told him. "Besides, you said *e*lected. This isn't an election, Sean."

"Oh, right. I should have said *se*lected, huh?"

"Yes, and if you'd shown it to me before you turned it in, I would have caught it."

"Well, okay, but it gets better, doesn't it?"

"Wrong," Tara replied. "It gets worse." Frowning at the paper, she went on reading. " 'I have lived in Tarenton all my life. It's a great town, and it's important to keep it that way, which is why I have volunteered my services at the Tarenton Elementary School Sports Clinic. In spite of this, I manage to maintain a B-plus average in high school and be a member of the Tarenton High Varsity Cheerleading Squad.' "

"So? What's wrong with that?"

"Everything!" Tara burst out. "For one, that's all you wrote, and it's too short. For two, you say 'in spite of' your volunteer work." She shook her head. "You make it sound like a handicap."

"Oh. I see what you mean." Sean laughed again. "Well, I did have something else on my mind when I wrote it," he said, thinking of Kate.

"That's not the point," Tara told him. "The point is, it's a lousy essay."

"Okay, okay, it's not my best work," Sean agreed. "But I'll be doing that dynamite routine again, remember? Once they see that, it'll knock that essay right out of their heads."

"Don't count on it," Tara warned him. "But speaking of your routine, I haven't heard you talk about practicing it lately."

"Well, I guess I haven't been," Sean admitted, pulling the car into the Garrison High parking lot. "But don't worry. It's still fresh. One good practice, that's all I need."

Sighing again, Tara stared at him. "Just tell me this, Sean," she said. "Do you want to go to Hawaii or not?"

"Sure I do." Reaching into the backseat, Sean pulled up his duffel bag and started checking to make sure he had everything he needed. "Of course, it won't be the end of the world if I don't go. In fact, I might have more fun if I stay right where I am. But don't worry, Tara," he said, opening his door, "I'll be fine Saturday night. You'll see."

Tara sat for a moment, alone in the car. It was obvious that Sean really didn't care much about Hawaii anymore, not with Kate in his life. Oh, sure, he'd go through with the contest, but his heart wouldn't be in it. His heart would be with Kate, and Kate was in Tarenton.

You just made a fool out of yourself, Tara thought. You practically bullied Sean about that essay just because you want to go to Hawaii, not because you want to go to Hawaii with *him*. It serves you right that he found Kate. Forget it, she told herself as she got out of the car. Put Hawaii out of your mind and find something else to think about.

It was easy enough to say, but it wasn't so easy to do. As Ardith Engborg watched from the sidelines, Tara, the only one of the cheerleaders who hadn't made a mistake lately, dropped a pompon, flubbed a cartwheel, tripped over her own feet, and went through the cheers with a frown on her face.

"What's the matter with you?" Olivia asked her, when they were taking a quick break. "Are you sick?"

Tara shook her head. "Sorry," she said, pushing her hair behind her ears. "I just can't seem to concentrate."

Hope smiled her first genuine smile in days. "I know exactly how you feel, Tara," she said. "Would you like to know what I've been doing about it?"

"I can't get much worse than this," Tara admitted.

"You have to use your imagination," Hope said. "And you have to imagine that if you don't do the cheer perfectly, the floor's going to open up and you'll drop into a pit full of broken violin strings."

Tara stared at her. "Violin strings?"

"Or snakes." Hope laughed. "Or spiders. Or whatever gives you nightmares. But you have to believe it," she warned. "Really believe it."

"That sounds almost as hard as doing the cheers right," Tara said. "But I'll try."

Not being particularly afraid of snakes or spiders, and not having any emotional attachment to violin strings, broken or otherwise, Tara had trouble imagining anything that would scare her into perfection. All she could come up with were a thousand Ardith Engborgs, screaming that she was the worst cheerleader ever born, and that she was off the squad.

It didn't work. Tara still couldn't concentrate, and during one of their simplest cheers, she turned left when she should have turned right, bumping into Peter, who was waiting to catch Jessica. Fortunately, Peter was able to adjust, and Jessica didn't land on the floor, but the thought that she could have was something that really did give Tara nightmares.

It didn't help, either, that Tarenton lost the game. Of course, they knew it would be close. After their last meeting, Garrison was out for blood, and they took the Wolves by surprise with

126

"Just because I dropped a pompon doesn't mean I don't support the team!"

"I'm not talking about one dropped pompon," Diana replied. "I'm talking about a lot of them. And a lot of falls and stumbles. Bill told me just last night that he doesn't feel you guys are behind the team anymore. And that hurts."

"Poor Bill! Tell him to play a better game and leave the cheerleading to us," Tara retorted.

"He's playing his best," Diana said. "But the squad isn't doing its best, and everybody can see it." She got up, smoothing her hair and adjusting her beautiful sweater. "The squad is just too sure of itself, that's why it's starting to slip. And if it slips much farther," she went on, smiling, "Coach Engborg will have to do something about it. She might even decide to get rid of the worst cheerleaders, the ones who keep on dropping their pompons. So look out, Tara. There are plenty of others waiting to take your place."

CHAPTER

"What's this all about?" Jessica asked Olivia, as the two of them walked up the curved path to the Armstrongs' white colonial house Wednesday evening. "Tara sounded like it was some kind of emergency."

Olivia nodded. "I know. She's worried about the squad." She rang the doorbell and leaned against a porch pillar to wait. "Tara likes to be dramatic, but this time, I think it's for real."

The door was opened by Marie, the Armstrongs' live-in housekeeper, who smiled and motioned the girls to go into the den. It was a large room, furnished with thick rugs and soft chairs, but just as Jessica and Olivia were about to make themselves comfortable, Tara burst into the room, a pencil in her mouth and a notepad tucked under her arm.

"Oh, good!" she said, running one hand through her curly red hair. "I was afraid you weren't coming. Sean couldn't make it, and I guess we all know why. But Hope and Peter said they'd be here. I wish they'd hurry up. I'll go get us something to drink while we're waiting."

"Wait a minute, Tara!" Olivia pushed herself out of the deep velvet wing chair. "Why don't you tell us what this is all about? What's the big secret?"

Tara laughed and sat down on the rug. "It's not a secret," she said, "and I would have told you everything over the phone, but I didn't have time."

"So tell us now," Jessica suggested.

"Let's wait for Peter and Hope," Tara said. "They should be here any minute."

"Together?" Olivia asked hopefully.

Tara shook her head and laughed again. "It was sneaky, I guess, but I didn't tell either of them that the other was coming." The doorbell rang and she hopped up. "Keep your fingers crossed that they didn't get here together, otherwise they might both decide to leave, and this is too important."

Fortunately, Hope and Peter arrived separately. Neither of them looked overjoyed to see the other, but once they were there, they were both too proud to be the one to go.

"Finally," Jessica said, as Tara set a tray of juice and cookies on the coffee table. "Let's get on with it. I've got homework to do."

"So do I," Tara told her, "but I'm willing to stay up a little later to do it. And I think after you hear what I have to say, you will, too." Taking a deep breath, she thought a second, and then

131

told them about her conversation with Diana.

"But that's not new," Olivia said when Tara had finished. "We all know Diana would try anything to get on the squad, including badmouthing us."

"But this time she's blaming us because the Wolves are losing," Tara argued.

"That ridiculous," Jessica said. "We have something to do with team spirit, but we're not responsible for every basket they don't make."

"Besides," Peter put in, "the Wolves aren't losing."

"Not yet," Hope said, without looking at him. "But if they lose Saturday night, they'll be tied for first place."

"Who do they play Saturday night?" Jessica asked.

"Deep River."

Everyone was quiet for a moment. Deep River was one of Tarenton's fiercest rivals. The Wolves hated to lose to anyone, but they especially hated losing to the Killers. And the cheerleaders knew that if any team had a chance of beating Tarenton, it was Deep River.

Olivia drank some juice, a frown on her face. "I really didn't realize it was that close," she said finally. "If Deep River has a chance of pushing Tarenton out of the race for the championship, they'll play harder than they've ever played before."

Jessica nodded. "They'd love to be the ones to knock the Wolves off their pedestal."

"And the Wolves keep going back and forth

132

going to talk to her. After all, she's the coach. If anybody can help us with this, she can."

"I'm surprised I didn't see it myself," Mrs. Engborg admitted when Olivia went to her office the next day. "I've been letting you rely on your standard cheers too long. No wonder you were getting stale."

"It *has* been a long time since we did something new," Olivia agreed. "I'm not trying to make excuses, though. We just got too sure of ourselves, like the Wolves. But if we work up a new cheer, it'll help us get back some of our old zip."

Their coach smiled. "You could certainly use it," she said frankly. "Now, let me see what you've come up with so far."

Olivia watched the coach as she studied the diagram the cheerleaders had made the day before. She nodded several times, and then she frowned.

Olivia laughed. "The pyramid, right?" she asked. "We knew you wouldn't like it, but we couldn't come up with anything else as exciting." She leaned toward Ardith Engborg's desk. "And it's got to be exciting. It's got to fly!"

"There are other ways to fly," the coach said dryly. "I know that pyramids are very common these days, but they're also dangerous." She chewed her pencil for a moment, then smiled at her captain. "But, as I said, there are other ways to fly and they can be exciting, too. Let me keep this. I should have something for you by this afternoon's practice."

135

The coach was as good as her word. When the six cheerleaders filed into the gym after school, she was already waiting for them, sitting on a low bleacher, making last-minute notes on a piece of paper.

"What's up?" Sean asked Tara as they warmed up. "The coach looks like she's all worked up about something."

"If you'd come to my house last night, you'd know," Tara said.

"Hey, give me a break," Sean protested with a laugh. "I took Kate home from the sports clinic and we got to talking." He grinned. "You know how it is."

Not lately, Tara thought. "Well, anyway," she said, "you'll find out soon enough. And you'd better not make any big plans with Kate until after Saturday night."

"All right," Coach Engborg said, clapping her hands. "I understand you want a fantastic routine to get yourselves and the Wolves back on track." She gave them a wry smile. "I can give it to you, but it's going to mean work, real work. We haven't got weeks, you know. We've got today, tomorrow, and Saturday morning. Three practices. That's it."

Sean groaned to himself. Tomorrow night was the final competition for Young Mr. Tarenton, and if he had to practice with the squad on Saturday morning, and cheer Saturday night, that left a total of about two hours to see Kate. He decided not to complain, though. He could tell the coach meant business.

136

"The first part of the routine is fine," their coach went on. "And I'm still working on words for the second part. It's the third part that's going to need the most work, so let's start with that. Sean, you and Peter kneel down side by side."

When Peter and Sean were in place, the coach had Jessica and Olivia climb into a standing position on their shoulders. The boys rose, their legs apart, and then Tara placed one foot on Sean's outside leg, and, hanging onto his free hand (the one that wasn't around Jessica's ankle), she pulled herself up until she was leaning at an angle, her arm outstretched, her pompon waving. On the other side, Hope did the same thing with Peter.

The six of them balanced there, trying not to wobble, while Coach Engborg studied them. It looked terrific, she thought, almost better than a pyramid. And of course, they weren't going to climb slowly into position. Jessica and Olivia would leap onto the boys' shoulders, while Tara and Hope would cartwheel their way across the floor and hop onto their legs. The move needed great concentration and split-second timing, and it wasn't going to be easy to accomplish — not in only three practices. But Ardith Engborg knew they could do it.

"Good," she said, and the cheerleaders broke apart. "Now, let's get to work."

"It's going to be great, isn't it?" Tara asked Sean as they headed for the locker rooms. Instead of feeling tired, which she normally would have after a rugged workout like that, she felt wonderful. For one thing, the squad was really alive again. She hadn't realized it, but they'd been doing most of their routines like sleepwalkers, so sure of their number-one position that they'd gotten cocky.

But more important, Tara felt as if *she* was alive again, and happy with herself. She'd counted on Sean to make something exciting happen, like the trip to Hawaii. But that had been a big mistake, and not just because he'd found Kate, either. What if he'd never met Kate? What if he'd won the contest and taken Tara to Hawaii? What then?

Nothing. She'd be right back where she started, relying on other people to make things happen for her. Now, though, *she* was the one making it happen. She'd been the one to get the squad to realize how close the Wolves were to losing, and it had been her idea to come up with a new routine. And it was working. That was exciting, and she'd done it by herself.

Of course, Diana did have something to do with it. If she'd kept her mouth shut, she might have gotten her wish and made it onto the squad. Too bad, Tara thought with a grin. Now she'll have to eat her words. The Wolves might still lose, but nobody could blame the squad, not after they saw the new routine.

"I think we're going to surprise everybody," she said to Sean now. "The fans have gotten just as used to our old routines as we have. Now they'll really have something to shout about, right?"

"Right," Sean agreed, checking the wall clock.

"I just hope when I cartwheel over, I don't wind up kicking you in the face," Tara laughed. "I never thought Coach Engborg would give us something so hard, but I guess she thinks we can do it."

"Right," Sean said again.

Tara looked at him. "You don't seem too excited about the whole thing," she remarked. "Now that I think about it, you actually looked bored while we were working on it."

"I'm not bored, Tara," Sean told her. "It's just not the best time in the world for me to be working on a new cheer, that's all. I've got a lot on my mind, and besides, the Wolves will win or lose without us."

"I can't believe you said that!" Tara stared at him, amazed and disgusted at the same time. "You know how important the squad is! You're the one who's always saying what a difference cheerleading makes to a team!"

Sean held up his hands, grinning and shaking his head. "Don't get all excited, okay?" he said. "I didn't mean it. I know we're important. And don't worry, I'll do my share of the work." Still smiling, he sauntered off to the locker room, leaving Tara alone in the hall.

Sure, she thought, he'll do his share of the work. But his heart's not going to be in it because his heart's with Kate. And if Sean isn't with us, *really* with us, that dynamite cheer is going to fizzle like a wet firecracker.

139

CHAPTER

B̲y Friday afternoon, Olivia was having the same thoughts about Hope and Peter. It wasn't that the two of them weren't interested in the cheer; they were. But they sure weren't interested in each other, and if somebody didn't do something about it, Olivia knew that the cheer would be the thing to suffer.

Whenever Hope or Peter had to do something alone, they were fine. Maybe their smiles weren't completely genuine, and maybe they were a fraction less enthusiastic than usual, but it was the kind of thing that only Coach Engborg would notice. And whenever she pointed it out, they changed immediately, becoming so friendly and energetic-looking that no one would ever have guessed they'd had to work at it.

But when they came together, Olivia thought, look out! Hope still got stiff and straight-backed, and Peter looked as if he wished the floor would open up and swallow him. Or maybe he wanted it to swallow Hope. Whichever it was, Olivia knew it wouldn't be long before the coach said something about it. And if she learned that personal problems were getting in the way of their cheering, she'd really let them have it. Not that she was unsympathetic, but when it came to good cheerleading, Ardith Engborg didn't let anything stand in the way.

"Can't you talk to Hope?" Jessica asked Friday afternoon after Tara and Hope had left the locker room. "She's usually so logical. If you tell her she's hurting the cheer, I bet she'll change."

"I tried talking to her," Olivia said.

"And?"

"Nothing." Olivia brushed her hair quickly, feeling frustrated. "She was nice and everything, but she absolutely refused to talk about Peter."

"Okay, so don't mention Peter," Jessica suggested. "Just concentrate on the cheer, and team spirit, and stuff like that. And don't forget to mention that Coach Engborg's going to be ready to spit nails pretty soon."

Olivia laughed. "Well, I guess I'll have to do something," she said. Then she shook her head. "How come I always get stuck with things like this?"

"Because you're the captain," Jessica said with a grin. "And the captain always does the dirty work."

Laughing again, Olivia tossed her towel at Jessica and the two of them left the locker room. It was nice to be able to joke about it, but she knew she really would have to talk to Hope soon, and maybe even Peter, too, if they didn't shape up. And that wasn't going to be funny at all.

"Well?" Kate said. "Are you ready?"

Sean nodded. "It's now or never."

The two of them were in Sean's car, heading for Tarenton Town Hall. It was Friday night, the night of the final competition for the Young Mr. Tarenton Contest. This time there would be only eleven boys to compete against, and even though Sean knew he stood a good chance against them, in spite of that lousy essay, he just didn't have the same feeling he'd had two weeks ago — that feeling of excitement and power, where he knew he was a winner and he couldn't do anything wrong.

Of course, he thought, glancing over at Kate, he was still a winner. A big winner. There was no amount of warm sand and sunny skies and blue-green waves that could make him feel the way Kate did.

"Listen," he said, pulling into the parking lot. "I've been thinking about it, and I've decided that if I win — "

"*If* you win?" Kate teased. "The last time I heard you talk about it, you had it all sewed up. What's the matter, are you losing confidence?"

"Me?" Sean laughed. "Never."

"Well, that's a relief," Kate said. "Don't let your head swell any more than it already is, but I kind of like your confidence. You wouldn't be you without it."

142

"Does that mean you won't tease me about it?"

"Hardly!" Kate laughed and squeezed his hand. "Teasing you is too much fun."

"Okay," he said, laughing, too. "Anyway, what I was going to say was *when* I win, I was thinking about giving the tickets to my father."

Kate stared at him, a surprised look in her brown eyes. "Why would you do that?"

Sean shrugged, trying to look as if it didn't matter. But it did. "Because I'd rather be here with you, that's why." He stared back at Kate, who still looked surprised. "What's the matter, don't you believe me?"

A smile appeared on her face, one of those mega-watt smiles that always made Sean want to leap into the air. "Of course I believe you," Kate said, leaning over to kiss him softly and quickly. "It's just that I think you'd be crazy to do it." She kissed him again, a little longer this time. "But don't let me stop you."

Even though there were fewer contestants, the size of the audience hadn't shrunk at all. Friends, relatives, and friends of relatives crowded into the hall, laughing and greeting each other, eager to see the crowning of the first Young Mr. Tarenton in the history of the town.

"There's Coach Engborg," Olivia said. "She told Sean she'd be here. I wonder what she'll say about his routine."

"She'll say he could use a little of that energy in our new cheer," Tara grumbled. "I can't believe how uninterested he is in it. And we've only got one more practice before the game. Does he really expect to get good overnight?"

"Knowing Sean, I'd say he does," David commented with a laugh. "Is he really not working on the cheer?"

"Oh, he's working," Tara said. "He's just not working hard."

"I hate to admit it, but I hadn't noticed," Jessica said. "I've been watching Peter and Hope. And they're almost working *too* hard, if that's possible."

"I know what you mean," Olivia told her. "They're like machines." Then she sighed. Time was running out. She'd have to talk to them, and since neither one of them was here tonight, she'd have to do it at tomorrow morning's practice.

"I don't even know what I'm doing here," Tara said, still feeling grumpy. "Sean doesn't care if I'm here. He doesn't care about anyone or anything but Kate."

"Where is Kate, anyway?" Olivia asked.

"Probably backstage," Jessica said, and settled into her seat as the houselights began to dim.

But Kate wasn't backstage. Sean didn't need anyone to hold his hand, and besides, as long as she was there, she wanted to see this thing from beginning to end.

So Kate was in the row in front of the cheerleaders, David, and Patrick, and before she'd realized who they were, she'd found herself listening to their conversation. Then, since she didn't want to embarrass them or herself, she'd kept quiet.

was sitting in front of them, put a finger to her lips and shook her head at Tara.

Tara half turned her head, and blushed when she saw Kate. Great, she thought. Now she probably thinks I'm just jealous or something. Maybe she didn't hear me, Tara thought.

Kate had heard her, but what she'd heard didn't bother her a bit. All it did was make her think some more and wish the contest would hurry up and be over. Sean had been wonderful, and she wanted to tell him so. But she also wanted to talk to him about a couple of other things, things that were much more important than the Young Mr. Tarenton Contest.

Finally, the talent acts were over, and the last part of the contest, the question and answer session, got started. Kate shifted restlessly in her seat, and Tara did, too, but for a different reason.

Tara dreaded this part, even though she didn't have a stake in the outcome anymore. But Sean's essay had been so bad, as far as she was concerned. And what if they made him read it out loud? If they did that, Tara thought, not a single person here would remember his fantastic routine.

Sean was slightly worried about this part, too. Too bad it didn't come before the talent portion, he thought, as he waited in the wings for his turn. If I could have done my routine last, nobody would remember a thing that came before it.

Much to Tara's relief, the contestants didn't have to read their essays in front of the audience. Instead, the MC would read part of one, and then

147

ask the writer something about what he'd said.

Unfortunately, the question Sean was asked didn't have anything to do with his grades, or his cheerleading, or his volunteer work. The MC, smiling the whole time, said, "Mr. Dubrow, you state here that you feel you should be Young Mr. Tarenton because you're young, you're from Tarenton, and you're a boy."

The audience had been expecting some kind of humble statement, so they were slow to react. But once they caught on, a laugh spread through the auditorium, small at first, but growing louder as more and more people joined in.

Sean listened to the laughter and tried to figure out what to do about it. If he answered seriously, they'd really think he was a fool. And if he laughed along with them, they might think he was embarrassed. He was, a little, he had to admit. It was one thing to write something, but it was another thing to have it read aloud in front of hundreds of people.

Then Sean caught sight of Kate. He hadn't spotted her before, but now he saw her. She was sitting tall and straight, and even though the lights were dim, he thought he saw a sparkle in her eyes. Kate was laughing, so why shouldn't he?

"Yes, sir," he said to the MC. "That's exactly what I wrote."

"Well, it certainly is true," the MC commented jovially, "But it's true of all the other contestants, too. So if everyone's equal, who should win?"

Sean took another look at Kate and then smiled back at the master of ceremonies. "That's a tough

148

question," he said. "I think I'll let the judges decide."

Even though his answers pleased the audience, they didn't please the judges. At least, they didn't please them enough. Because when the contest was over, Sean Dubrow was still young, still from Tarenton, and still a boy. But he wasn't Young Mr. Tarenton.

"Well?" Kate said as they drove away. "How do you feel?"

"How do *you* feel?" Sean asked.

"Great," she said. "I had a good time and I saw this guy do the most fabulous gymnastic routine I've ever seen."

"Yeah?" Sean grinned, happy that she'd liked it.

"Except on television, of course," Kate went on. "In the Olympics, you know."

"Of course," Sean agreed with a laugh.

"So how do you feel?" she asked again. "Disappointed?"

"A little," he admitted. "I guess I blew it with that essay."

Kate nodded. "Probably. I think they wanted someone a little more serious." She turned sideways in her seat and peered at him over the tops of her glasses. "You weren't really serious about that contest, were you?"

"I was until I met you," Sean told her. "And it wasn't that I didn't care. It's just that I cared more about you, and I couldn't concentrate on anything else." He pulled the car to a stop in front of her house and put his arm around her. "Now I don't have to concentrate on anything else," he said, kissing her.

Kate enjoyed the kiss, but finally she pulled her head away. "Yes, you do," she said. "You have to concentrate on cheerleading. Remember when I bet you that change that the Wolves just might not make the championship?"

Sean nodded.

"I've been following the scores, you know," she went on. "And if they don't win tomorrow night, they're going to be tied for first with Deep River. Once Deep River gets that close, they'll be hard to stop."

"Seems to me I've heard this before," Sean said, remembering Tara.

"Well, you haven't been listening," Kate told him. "I know I told you that I don't really follow cheerleading, but I happen to know that the Tarenton cheerleading squad is the best. They could make a big difference to the Wolves, if they wanted to."

Sean laughed. "Okay, okay," he said. "I confess. My mind has not been on cheerleading. But it will be now, I promise. After all, I don't want to lose that bet."

"Good. Because I don't want to win it. So start concentrating." Kate laughed, too, and then pulled him close. "But you can wait until tomorrow," she whispered. "Right now, you can concentrate on me."

CHAPTER

 15

Practice had been called for nine-thirty on Saturday morning. The squad usually didn't work out on the same day they had a game, but because their cheer was so new and so important, they would have been willing to work clear up to game time on it.

Coach Engborg had other ideas, though. "You can't afford to get worn out," she said as they gathered in the gym. "You might give it everything you've got this morning and have nothing left tonight."

"Impossible," Sean said confidently. "In fact, I can guarantee you, Coach, that I will have plenty left tonight, no matter what we do right now."

The others shook their heads, amused by Sean's attitude, and even their coach smiled. "Well, you did promise me that your routine for the contest would be one of the best things I've ever seen you do," she remarked, "and you kept your promise. I was very impressed, Sean."

Sean's mouth opened in surprise. Praise like that from the coach was worth its weight in gold. "Thanks, Coach," he said gratefully.

But for Ardith Engborg, it was time to move on to other things. "Now," she told the cheerleaders, "what we'll do this morning are the first and second parts of the cheer, and we'll go all out on them. But I just want you to walk through the last part."

"But Coach Engborg." Tara looked worried. "That's the hardest part, and we haven't done it right yet." She hadn't been kidding when she'd told Sean she was afraid of kicking him in the face. "I'd feel a lot better if we forgot the first and second parts and just did the last one."

"I would, too," Hope agreed. "I'm still not sure of myself on that."

"I think the coach is right," Peter said to no one in particular. "Sometimes it helps if you don't concentrate on something that gives you a lot of trouble. While you're not worrying about it, it just might go all right."

Hope looked deliberately away from him, and Olivia raised her eyes to the ceiling. Couldn't they at least call a truce just long enough to get through tonight's game? Then they could pick up the battle where they left off.

"I understand why you want to work on that," Coach Engborg said to Hope and Tara. "But trust me. You've got the moves down, and now you need a little distance from them. A walk-through will be enough." She clapped her hands briskly. "Let's go, from the top!"

As Olivia and Jessica took their positions, Sean joined Tara on the sidelines. She still looked worried.

"Hey," he said, "didn't you hear what the coach said? Trust her." He grinned. "And if you can't trust her, trust me. I'll be there, and I'm not about to let you break my nose."

Tara looked at him. "What's gotten into you?" she asked.

"What do you mean?"

"Yesterday you couldn't have cared less about this cheer. 'What's the big deal?' you said. 'The Wolves can take care of themselves.' "

"Did I really say that?"

Tara nodded. "And when you didn't win the contest, I thought for sure you'd come in here this morning with your mouth down to here." She indicated a spot two inches off the floor. "So what happened?"

"Well, I have to admit, I was a little disappointed at not winning last night," Sean told her. "But after all, a trip to Hawaii is just a short-term pleasure. And since I'll probably be a cheerleader for quite a while, I thought I'd better start concentrating on it." He laughed at the incredulous expression on her face. "Come on, Tara, you know I care about the squad. Besides," he said, leaning close, his dark eyes twinkling, "don't tell the coach, but I have a bet on tonight's game. If the Wolves win, I'll be thirty-eight cents richer!"

Tara didn't know what he was talking about,

153

but she found herself laughing along with him. For whatever reason, Sean's heart was back with the squad, and as long as it was, the cheer was that much closer to being great.

"Who's the best?
Tarenton!
Ahead of the rest?
Tarenton!
We don't jest,
Tarenton's best!
Yea, Tarenton!"

There was a big cheer from the audience, but not quite as big as it would have been if the game was being played at home. Plenty of Tarenton fans had come to Deep River High, but the Killers' fans had been streaming into the gym since late afternoon.

The game had been underway for twenty minutes, and already everyone could tell it was going to be close. The Tarenton and Deep River teams were both up for it. They knew how much was riding on it, and both were determined to come out the winner.

"This isn't going to be easy," Jessica gasped as the squad ran to the sidelines. "I feel like we're rowing upstream."

"It's more like a treadmill," Sean said, wiping his face with a towel. "We get a basket, they get a basket. One step forward and one step backward."

"At least the fans are being decent," Tara

commented. "I was afraid the ones from Deep River would come armed with ripe tomatoes."

"Nah," Sean told her. "They appreciate good cheerleading when they see it, and they're seeing it from us. That's why they're being decent."

Olivia fluffed out her hair with her fingers and frowned. Maybe the fans were being decent, but Hope and Peter sure weren't. It was the same old thing — cold looks and cold shoulders. She was getting very tired of it. She couldn't do anything about it now, though. Deep River had just made another basket.

"Come on," she said. "Let's get back out there and let the Wolves know we're here!"

The applause for Deep River's basket was still going strong as the Tarenton squad streamed onto the floor. Their fans saw them and began waving red and white banners and making as much noise as possible, hoping to drown out the other side.

> "Okay, Wolves,
> Now's your chance
> To let Deep River know
> It's met its match!
> Sink one now!
> Sink it fast!
> Go ahead, Wolves!
> Have a blast!"

The fans screamed, the cheerleaders cheered, and the Wolves did their best to sink one. The excitement in the gym crackled like electricity, and so did the feeling between Hope and Peter. On

155

the line, "Have a blast!" Peter was supposed to lift Hope by the waist, just as Sean was doing with Tara. Sean lifted Tara high into the air, but Peter was slightly off balance as he went into the lift, and he staggered. Not much, but enough for Hope to go up at a slant. When he set her down, she pulled away from him sharply.

No one seemed to have noticed, certainly not the Killers. Instead, they got the ball, and three seconds later, they got another basket. Now they were ahead by four points.

Olivia had had it. Not with the Wolves — they were playing like demons — but with Hope and Peter. As the squad gathered on the sidelines, she turned to them, her eyes blazing.

"Listen," she said, still breathing hard from the cheer, "I don't know what the problem is between you two anymore, and right now I don't care. What I care about now is doing our best, and that means all of us. Halftime's coming up and if you keep on going the way you have been, you're going to blow that cheer."

Olivia took another deep breath and put her hands on her hips. She was small, tiny almost, but when she was mad, her size was the last thing anybody noticed. "And if you ruin that cheer," she warned, "after all the work the rest of us have put into it, then you don't belong on this squad anymore."

It wasn't the talk she'd had in mind, but there was no time to be nice and sympathetic at that moment. In fact, there was no time for anything except another short cheer before halftime. For-

156

tunately, it didn't involve any contact between Hope and Peter, so it went well. But when the buzzer sounded, the Wolves were still behind, 54–50.

The squad had a few minutes before they gave their new cheer, and they spent it out in the hall, sipping water and trying not to be nervous. When Coach Engborg joined them, she smiled encouragingly. "It's going to go fine," she said. "Just concentrate on what you're doing and block out everything around you, and you can't miss." She stopped, looked around, and then asked sharply, "Where are Peter and Hope?"

"Down there," Olivia said, nodding toward the end of the hall. "I guess they had something to discuss."

The coach frowned. "I hope it's a short something," she remarked, and then went back into the gym.

It wasn't a short something, of course, and it would need a lot of discussion before Hope and Peter got it worked out, but for the first time in almost two weeks, they were actually talking.

Hope had started it. Walking up to Peter at the water fountain, she'd touched his arm, almost afraid that he'd pull away from her.

But Peter didn't pull away. There was no anger in Hope's face when he turned from the water fountain, and her hand, he realized, felt just right.

"Peter," she'd said, "Olivia has every right to be furious with us. We have to try to forget what's happened, for tonight, at least."

"I know." Peter smiled tentatively. "I know we deserved it. I'm just surprised she didn't haul off and slug us."

Hope smiled, too. Then she realized that she still had her hand on his arm. "I'd like to be able to forget what's happened for longer than just tonight," she said. "I've been . . . I've been stubborn. I'm sorry."

"So have I," Peter admitted, wanting to touch her and not quite sure whether he should. "I got used to being mad, I guess, and it's hard to change."

"Have you?" Hope asked. "Changed, I mean?"

Peter nodded slowly. "I think I have," he said. "What about you?"

"Yes," she told him. "It's funny, but I think I stayed angry for so long because if I stopped being mad, that would mean I'd stopped caring about you." She reached out and touched his arm again. "And I haven't stopped caring about you, Peter."

Peter took her other hand and pulled her closer to him. "I haven't stopped caring, either, Hope," he said as he kissed her.

"Hey, you two!" Sean let out a whistle from the other end of the hall. "Save it for later. Right now, we've got some heavy cheering to do!"

With a laugh, Hope and Peter joined the rest of the squad, and to the sound of stamping feet and wildly clapping hands, the six cheerleaders raced into the gym.

The crowd quieted as Hope and Peter, Tara and Sean stood on the sides, their pompons held aloft, their heads turned toward the two gymnasts of the squad. Jessica and Olivia were standing in the center, hands on their hips, and as the others swung the pompons down, they broke into simultaneous forward handsprings that carried them to the edge of the cheering crowd.

Another swoop of the pompons, and the two girls moved backward in slow, graceful walkovers. At the center of the floor again, they stretched out their arms until their hands were touching, then with a push, seemed to send each other sideways into a series of cartwheels that took them all around the edges of the stands. As they neared the center again, the rest of the squad was waiting, and together the six of them formed a line.

Next came the dance portion of the cheer, accompanied by words that the Tarenton fans picked up immediately.

"Listen, Deep River,
Listen close,
The Tarenton Wolves
Will never coast!
They've got the power
And they've got the drive
The Tarenton Wolves are still alive!
Yea, Tarenton!"

The cheerleaders went through it again, with the fans chanting along, and then it was time for the third part of the cheer.

Breaking out of the line, the four girls ran to their positions, while Sean and Peter knelt in the

159

center. From behind them, Jessica and Olivia put themselves into motion, springing forward until they were suddenly standing on the boys' shoulders. Before the crowd had a chance to react, Tara and Hope came cartwheeling across from the sides. Tara didn't kick Sean in the face, and with a smile of pure happiness, Hope reached for Peter's hand and pulled herself up. They'd done it. They'd done it perfectly, and fans of both schools erupted in shouts and whistles and applause that shook the stands and reverberated around the gym.

"I think," Sean said, as they ran out of the gym to make way for the Deep River cheerleading squad, "that that is going to be one hard act to follow."

Olivia laughed, hugging Hope and Peter and anybody else who came close to her. "That felt great!" she shouted. "Let's do it again!"

"I've got a better idea," Jessica said, laughing, too. "Let's just rewrite the words and do it for when the Wolves play for the championship. Because if that cheer didn't get them going, nothing will."

Whether it was the cheer that got them going, the Wolves themselves, or a combination of both, nobody knew, and nobody really cared. All they knew or cared about was that when the final buzzer sounded, an exhausted but triumphant Tarenton team had beaten Deep River by a score of 82–78.

Kate was waiting for Sean outside the boys'

locker room, her hair frizzed even more than usual from running her fingers through it during the tense game. Her glasses were slipping and smudged, of course, but they couldn't hide the light in her eyes.

"That had to be one of the best games I've ever seen," she said, giving him a hug.

"It was exciting, I'll say that," Sean agreed. "And how about the squad, huh? Don't you have a good word for us?"

"The squad?" Kate pretended to be confused. "Oh, you mean the ones in the red and white uniforms running around and yelling?" She grinned. "They were fantastic," she said, "especially the guy with the dark blond hair and dark eyes. I wouldn't mind getting to know him."

Sean put his arm around her waist. "I think I can arrange an introduction," he told her.

Kate laughed and then took his hand, turning it palm up. "Here," she said, and dropped thirty-eight cents into it. "You won the bet, fair and square."

Pushing her glasses up, Sean bent his head and kissed her, ignoring the rest of the people swirling around them.

"Hey," Olivia said, as she and David came up to them. "Sorry to interrupt, but the rest of us are going to the Pizza Palace to celebrate. Are you guys coming?"

Sean nodded. "Why not?" he said, never taking his eyes off Kate. "I'm a rich man now."

What can possibly get the old squad and the new squad together? Read Cheerleaders #32, TO-GETHER AGAIN.

The Stepsisters

#1

The War Between the Sisters

by Tina Oaks

Chapter Excerpt

Paige Whitman unzipped the plastic cover that held the dress she was to wear to her father's wedding. She had put off looking at the dress until the very last minute. When she learned the dress would be pink, she had groaned. There were colors she loved, colors she could take or leave alone, and then there was pink, which hated her as much as she hated it!

And the style was as impossible for her as the color. She didn't even have to try the dress on to know how it would look. At sixteen she was taller than most of her friends, and thinner without being really skinny. But taller meant longer, and she knew her neck was too long to wear a low, rounded neckline like that.

Paige's instinct was to wail. Dresses were supposed to do things *for* you, not *to* you. The only tiny comforting thing she could think of was that Katie Summer Guthrie, her fifteen-year-old step-sister-to-be would be wearing a matching monstrosity. Even though pink was a blonde's color, not even Katie could look like anything in *that* dress. It was comforting that she wouldn't be alone in her humiliation.

Beyond the other bed in the hotel room they shared, Paige's ten-year-old sister Megan hummed happily as she put on her own dress. Megan was a naturally happy-go-lucky girl, but Paige had never seen her as excited as she had been since their father announced his coming marriage to Virginia Mae Guthrie. Her father had tried to control his own excitement and tell them about his bride-to-be in a calm, sensible way. But Paige knew him too well to be fooled, and anyway he gave himself dead away!

He started by telling them how he had met Virginia Mae on a business trip to Atlanta, then how beautiful she was. He went from that to her divorce five years before and how she had been raising her three children alone ever since. Paige almost giggled. Here was William Whitman, whose logic and cool courtroom delivery were legendary in Philadelphia legal circles. Yet he was jumping around from one subject to another as he talked about Virginia Mae.

Paige had driven down to Atlanta with her father and Megan earlier in the summer so the children could meet. Paige had agreed that Virginia Mae Guthrie was as lovely as she was gentle.

Paige had tried to shrug away the twinge of resentment that came when she thought of Katie Summer. The girl had to be putting on an act. *Nobody* could possibly be as lighthearted and happy as she pretended to be. And nobody would be that pretty in a fair world. Seventeen-year-old Tucker seemed like a nice enough guy, although his exaggerated good manners threw Paige off a little. Ten-year-old Mary Emily was cute. But it was awkward to be the only one holding back when her father and Megan were both so obviously deliriously happy.

Her father made the marriage plans sound so simple: "Right after our wedding, Virginia and the children will move up here to Philadelphia. We'll all be one big happy family together."

Paige had said nothing then or since, but concealing her doubts hadn't made them go away. She hated feeling like a sixteen-year-old grouch, but it just didn't make sense that everything would work out that easily. Not only would there be more than twice as many people in the same house as before, but the people themselves would be different.

Even if people from the south didn't think differently than people from the north, they certainly *sounded* different when they talked. And the Guthries were as completely southern as Paige's family was northern. Mrs. Guthrie and her three children had lived in Atlanta all their lives.

Megan giggled and fluffed out her full skirt. "Isn't it great? I can't wait to show this dress back home."

Back home. Philadelphia meant only one person to Paige . . . Jake Carson. She shuddered at the thought of Jake seeing her in that pink dress. She would die, just simply die where she stood, if he ever saw her looking this gross.

She sighed and fiddled with the neck of the pink dress, wishing she hadn't even thought of Jake. Simply running his name through her mind was enough to sweep her with those familiar waves of almost physical pain. It didn't make sense that loving anyone could be so painful. But just the memory of his face, his intense expression, the brooding darkness of his thoughtful eyes was enough to destroy her self-control.

But even when Jake looked at her, he was absolutely blind to who she really was. She knew what he thought: that she was a nice kid, that she was fun to talk to, that she was William Whitman's daughter. Period. He didn't give the slightest indication that he even realized that she was a girl, much less a girl who loved him with such an aching passion that she couldn't meet his eyes for fear he might read her feelings there.

Megan caught Paige around the waist and clung to her. "Sometimes I get scared, thinking about the changes. It *is* going to be wonderful, isn't it, Paige?" Megan's voice held the first tremulous note of doubt Paige had heard from her sister.

"Absolutely wonderful," Paige assured her, wishing she felt as much confidence as she put into her tone.

Even as she spoke, she saw Jake's face again, his dark eyes intent on hers as he had talked to her about the wedding. "Look at your dad," Jake had said. "Anything that makes him that happy has to be a lucky break for all of you."

She had nodded, more conscious of how lucky she was to be with Jake than anything else.

Jake had worked around their house in Philadelphia for about a year and a half. Paige didn't believe in love at first sight, but it had almost been that way with her. From the first day, she found herself waiting breathlessly for the next time he came to work. She found herself remembering every word he said to her, turning them over and over in her mind later. It wasn't that he was mysterious. It was more that she always had the sense of there being so much more in his mind than he was saying. She was curious about him, his life, his friends, how he thought about things. In contrast to a lot of people who smiled easily and laughed or hummed when they worked, he was silent and withdrawn unless he was talking with someone.

Before he came, she hadn't realized how painful it was to love someone the way she did Jake. She hadn't asked to fall in love with him or anybody. She had even tried desperately to convince herself that he wasn't different from other boys, just nicer and older. That didn't work because it wasn't true. Jake really was different from the boys she knew at school. Although he talked enough when he had something to say, he was mostly a little aloof without being awkward and shy. And he wasn't an ordinary kind of handsome. His features were strong, with firm cheekbones; deeply set eyes; and a full, serious mouth.

167

Maybe one day she would quit loving him as quickly as she had begun. But even thinking about that happening brought a quick thump of panic in her chest. Knowing how it felt to be so much in love, how could she bear to live without it?

Later, when the wedding march began and the doors of the little chapel were opened, Paige was overwhelmed with the strange feeling that she was watching all this from a distance. Even as she walked beside Katie Summer and kept careful time to the music, she didn't feel as if she was a part of what was happening.

Paige felt a touch against her arm and looked over at Katie Summer. Katie flashed her a quick, sly smile that brought a fleeting dimple to her cheek. Paige swallowed hard, ducked her head, and looked away. Later she would have to deal with this girl, but not now, not while her father was repeating the same vows he had made so many years before to her own mother.

But that quick glance had been enough to remind her of how wrong she had been about how Katie Summer would look in her matching pink dress. It made Paige feel leggy and graceless beside her.

All the Guthries were good-looking. Tucker was almost as tall as Paige's father, and comfortingly nice to look at in a different, curly-haired way. Mary Emily, behind with Megan, was button cute. But the girl at Paige's side was just too much! Katie's thick, dark blonde curls spilled in glorious profusion around her glowing face.

Her pink dress picked up the rosiness of her deep tan and showed off the sparkle of her laughing blue eyes. Paige held her head high, fighting a sudden feeling of inadequacy that made her breath come short.

Looking back, Paige was sure that the wedding brunch was as beautiful as any meal she would ever eat. As they ate, Grandma Summer bent to Paige to make conversation, her soft voice rising in an exciting, different rhythm. "Virginia Mae tells me you play the piano, Paige, and that you're an excellent student. My, I know your father is just *so* proud of you."

Before Paige could reply, Katie flipped her glowing head of curls, turned away, and put her hand on Paige's father's arm. "I just had a perfectly *terrifying* thought," she said, looking up into his face. "My goodness, I hope you don't expect *me* to have a lot of talent or be a bookworm. I've got to tell you right off that I don't believe in all that."

After an astonished look, Paige's father covered Katie's hand with his, and chuckled. "That's pretty interesting," he said. "What *do* you believe in, Katie Summer?"

Her laugh was quick and soft. "Having a *wonderful* time, just like I am today."

Naturally he beamed at her. Who could help it when everything she said sounded so intimate and appealing in that soft, coaxing drawl? Paige felt a shiver of icy jealousy. That Katie Summer was something else!

They're talented....They're winners....

CHEERLEADERS®

They're the hottest squad in town!

Don't miss any of these exciting CHEERLEADERS® books!
Order today!   **$2.25 U.S./$2.95 CAN.**

- ☐ 33402-6 **#1 TRYING OUT** Caroline B. Cooney
- ☐ 33403-4 **#2 GETTING EVEN** Christopher Pike
- ☐ 33404-2 **#3 RUMORS** Caroline B. Cooney
- ☐ 33405-0 **#4 FEUDING** Lisa Norby
- ☐ 33406-9 **#5 ALL THE WAY** Caroline B. Cooney
- ☐ 33407-7 **#6 SPLITTING** Jennifer Sarasin
- ☐ 33687-8 **#7 FLIRTING** Diane Hoh
- ☐ 33689-4 **#8 FORGETTING** Lisa Norby
- ☐ 33705-X **#9 PLAYING GAMES** Jody Sorenson Theis
- ☐ 33815-3 **#10 BETRAYED** Diane Hoh
- ☐ 33816-1 **#11 CHEATING** Jennifer Sarasin
- ☐ 33928-1 **#12 STAYING TOGETHER** Diane Hoh
- ☐ 33929-X **#13 HURTING** Lisa Norby
- ☐ 33930-3 **#14 LIVING IT UP** Jennifer Sarasin
- ☐ 40047-9 **#15 WAITING** Jody Sorenson Theis
- ☐ 40048-7 **#16 IN LOVE** Carol Stanley
- ☐ 40187-4 **#17 TAKING RISKS** Anne Reynolds
- ☐ 40188-2 **#18 LOOKING GOOD** Carol Ellis
- ☐ 37816-3 **CHEERLEADERS BOXED SET**
  Four Titles: **#1 Trying Out, #2 Getting Even, #3 Rumors**
  and **#4 Feuding** (Not available in Canada)   **$9.00**
- ☐ 40189-0 **#19 MAKING IT** Susan Blake
- ☐ 40190-4 **#20 STARTING OVER Super Edition** Patricia Aks and Lisa Norby
  $2.50 U.S./$3.50 CAN.

Scholastic Inc.
P.O. Box 7502, East McCarty Street, Jefferson City, MO 65102

Please send me the books I have checked above. I am enclosing $_____
(please add $1.00 to cover shipping and handling). Send check or money order—no cash or
C.O.D.'s please.

Name_____

Address_____

City_____State/Zip_____
Please allow four to six weeks for delivery. Offer good in U.S.A. only. Sorry, mail order not available
to residents of Canada.   CHE862

TRUE LOVE! CRUSHES! BREAKUPS! MAKEUPS!

Find out what it's like
to be a COUPLE.